I0538660

# The Electrics
## // HARRISON KAVANAUGH

**WHITE BISON PRESS**
First Edition, February 2013

ISBN: 0615764622
ISBN-13: 978-0615764627

*For my parents Michael and Debra*
*and my brother Zachary*

# 1

Eliza Gershwin gazes out the window of her family's large New England beachside home, waves crashing on snow dusted sand a hundred yards before her. It is a particularly cool fall day and her thoughts are distant and clouded. Since childhood, she has felt that the weather reflects her state of mind. It is only ever as clear as she. Today, the sky is grey and ambiguous.

Every creak and shudder of the warm, incandescently lit house brings her ears to immediate attention, pulling ever closer those far and fearful thoughts. Her parents are out, and she has been asked to receive a very important and unusual delivery for her father. She waits in silent unease for the sound of the door.

Eliza's father, Steve Gershwin, is a real estate developer with twice as many dollars to his name as he has seconds remaining to live, should his life continue for another fifty years. Real estate, he confesses, is not his passion, but a "means to his dreams". Dreams of which generally include voicing his beliefs and putting his great sums of money where his mouth is. Politically and socially, he is a man of profound influence.

When the U.S. Government first proposed a large-scale production of Electric warriors to take the place of human soldiers, Steve Gershwin opposed the movement publicly. From what his generation had seen, tampering with nature rarely bodes well. Moral dilemma aside, the environmental repercussions of such manufacture could be enormous. He also feared that the compact CryoFusion power plants in each Electric could release dangerous levels of radiation if their structures were compromised in battle.

However, Gershwin's substantial efforts were no match for the ideas that the government proposed. Even if the new CryoFusion devices were not as perfectly safe as advertised, the public overwhelmingly favored sending out Electrics to replace their own children on the battlefield.

After the war concluded and Human Incorporated began to develop the first line of Electrics for domestic operation, CEO Henry Sharpe knew that winning Gershwin over would make for a much smoother ride (though he already possessed essential government support, considering the sizable economic boost promised by Electric labor). With a great deal of convincing from both Sharpe and the U.S. Government, Gershwin reluctantly consented to receiving one of the very first Human Electric beings.

Eliza glances at the calendar on the kitchen wall. It glows blue and dull, reading: *11.19.2097*. For more than six months, Eliza had been inundated by advertisements projecting a forthcoming seismic social shift on this date. The official release of the Human Electrics.

This morning, she had watched via live news stream as the final design was revealed in Time Square. When the two glossy white doors parted on stage, Eliza thought that a man had stepped out from them. A handsome man with a clear face and clear eyes, dressed in a white cotton jumpsuit. It walked naturally and stepped evenly, approaching the podium with a poised form of organic movement that, in a human, one would associate with confidence.

Eliza and viewers across the world were instantly rendered breathless. What they saw did not appear to be a technological marvel ten years ahead of anything out today—though it was exactly that. There was no titanium alloy to be seen, no glossy polycarbonate, protruding wires, lights, or anything vaguely mechanical. This being bore no resemblance to its military-purposed predecessors, who were often referred to by the derogatory term "robot". By far, the most shocking aspect of its appearance was that there was nothing shocking at about it. The being simply looked like a man. Albeit, a man is his ideal form.

Those unsettling images continue to flicker through Eliza's thoughts, having been burned clearly into her mind by her family's

Pixeflux television, a sporty new piece of technology capable of recreating a three dimensional image with photonic accuracy. She cannot help but associate the Electric's startlingly lifelike appearance with the label of "man". But it is not, she tries to think. It is a machine. Just a machine, created by man. Still, her logic and reason are hardly a match for what her eyes have informed her. But her mind persists. That is not skin, but a shear-resistant silicone blend—she once read—semi-opaque with muted crimson undertones. There is no blood in its veins, but hydraulic fluid and antifreeze. It has no heart and no mind, but a compact CryoFusion power plant and an array of molecular chips. Those eyes do not reflect a soul, but simply draw in light through synchronized Pixeflux cameras. If anything, they would reflect a bit of elegant programming, and nothing more. He is not a human. *It* is not a human. But still, some part of her will not accept those words.

A knock echoes through the house and Eliza jolts upright, thoughts scattered by a primitive response to the jarring auditory stimulus. One of the shutters has come unfastened in the wind, and now flaps loudly against the house. Her nerves begin to settle as her heartbeat slows to normal. The capacity to reason returns.

Eliza removes a loop of steel garden wire from the kitchen junk drawer and cuts a small piece to fasten the broken shutter. Neither of her busy parents have taken the time to repair it properly, and since the house staff are off for the day, she decides to impose a temporary fix of her own.

She steps outside to tie the wire around the broken brass latch, fastening the other end to the corresponding hardware on the house.

Though hardly more than a minute has passed, her hands have already grown cold and numb. But before she can step inside to warm up, the sound of approaching tires drives a chill up her spine. She turns to notice a sleek, immaculately white delivery van making its way toward the house. It is unmarked, with the exception of five grey uppercase letters written cleanly on either side.

# 2

As the pair of red taillights trace their way back down the drive and through the haze, the unusual exchange hangs on Eliza like a sleepless night's dream. The humanoid machine now standing beside her had been unconscious and devoid of even the subtlest movement only moments ago. But now she is afraid to turn, fearing another glimpse of the Electric's otherworldly, yet lifelike eyes.

She swipes her fingers across the pages of a digital booklet. According to the driver, it is something like a user agreement. Something like one, but not quite—his smug smile informed her. Eliza wonders if this collection of documents might be the controversial contract that sent ripples through the consciousness of social media. But for now, there are more pressing matters at hand. Like what the hell she is supposed to do with an electric man. Invite it inside for a drink of water, or plug it in somewhere to charge?

Before Eliza is able to string together a suitable sentence in her mind, let alone speak it, a sound emanates from the Electric. A sound not dissimilar from the type produced by a human voice. However, with much richer tones, and suffused with a concentrated dose of thought. Each vowel and consonant perfectly formed, without a single inadvertent vibration. Not one placeholder "like" or "um", each syllable and pause chosen to fulfill a very specific purpose. Pure speech, pure communication, eliciting nothing but the intended emotional and intellectual response in the listener.

"I will not take offense, whether you address me as a man or a toaster oven."

Eliza's face is charmed into a smile, her heavy mood lightened. Of all the high technology she's dealt with, not a single gadget has come preprogrammed with an icebreaker. This thought fills her mind and she giggles aloud, partly in surprise, and partly in a cathartic release long overdue. Tension is dispersed through a gentle abdominal convulsion, expulsion of breath, and vibration of sound. Laughter.

She invites the Electric inside, habitually uttering a halting command, much like what one would offer to voice recognition software.

"Come inside."

The Electric's processors take in this utterance among a sea of other auditory and visual data gathered by omnifrequency microphones and motion sensitive Pixeflux cameras, send it all instantly and anonymously to the cloud, receive instant feedback based on comparisons with previously catalogued human behavioral data, choose a corresponding physiomechanical response, which in this case involves triggering an array of valves in 22 of the 48 nanohydraulic bundles located in Core Region 5 (CR5), each bundle tugging gently and specifically at the CR5 silicone composite tissue, producing the expression of a human smile. The smile corresponds to data informing the Electric that the human does not yet trust it, and that the human still possesses a cognitive dissonance relating to the Electric's identity and social standing.

Prior this phsyiomechanical response, a secondary independent processor had also run the cloud data through a proprietary algorithmic loop, SyncAlg, perfusing the Electric's system with a wave of abstract emotional data. Through SyncAlg, the Electric registered the guardedness of the human as endearing. This emotion was then coded, synced with the cloud, and the Electric was informed of new behavior catering to its SyncAlg result. Thus, the smile.

The next results prompt the Electric to engage in the complex pattern of movement required to take a single step. It follows Eliza inside.

# 3

"How does this work?"

The two stand in the kitchen, Eliza leaning against the counter and sipping at a glass of water not to quench a thirst, but to quench a nervous energy with action. The Electric's arms hang readily by its sides, posture upright and lenses wide as it catalogs every detail of its new surroundings.

Eliza's inquiry is processed, and the Electric receives data from a portion of the cloud containing a copy of the digital booklet handed to Eliza by the driver.

"I require nothing more than what you would provide a human guest. Perhaps even less."

"Do you need to be charged?"

"My power source will sustain me for the duration of my animation cycle."

A shiver runs up Eliza's spine as she recalls the potential power sources discussed by speculators. Human has avoided discussing the technical specifics, but considering the chargeless one-hundred-year animation cycle they advertise, outside experts have reduced the possibilities to only a couple technologies possessing that capability. None of which have been generally adopted, for safety reasons.

"What is your power source?"

The Electric lifts one silicone arm—nanohydraulic bundles pulling soundlessly at titanium skeletal elements—and indicates its chest.

"An atomic reaction between anticarbon and the carbon portion of atmospheric $CO_2$. The anticarbon supply and reactor are encased in nillium, an antimatter-neutral substance. Each reaction destroys both the anticarbon and carbon atoms, releasing an enormous amount of heat that is instantaneously converted to electricity. Since there is no excess heat, the process has been named CryoFusion. Though that nomenclature is not entirely accurate."

Eliza can't help but stare at the Electric's human-looking chest, trying to grasp how beneath the white cotton fabric, silicone flesh, and titanium alloy occurs an immensely powerful and dangerous reaction. Like a walking, talking, atomic bomb, she fears.

"If you are comfortable, feel my breath."

Eliza is caught off-guard.

"What?"

"Place your hand here."

Much to Eliza's surprise, her feet step forward and her arm reaches up to the mouth of the manlike machine. The Electric exhales and she reels back in shock.

"You're breathing!?"

The Electric smiles.

"That is oxygen byproduct, warmed in the CryoFusion reaction."

If it speaks truthfully, the mechanical being before her more closely demonstrates the impossibility of perpetual motion than any machine she has yet to see.

"All you ever have to do is breathe?"

"I must also take in a synthetic blend of coolant and hydraulic fluid when my levels are low, but my only external energy requirement is atmospheric carbon dioxide. It is the most environmentally sound technology available today. However, unlike traditional chemical reactions, matter is destroyed in mine. If I were to run indefinitely, theoretically, I would consume the universe. But in the short term, Electrics will increase the concentration of oxygen in Earth's atmosphere. Better technology will surely be developed to replace this one before it causes significant damage."

Eliza is dumbstruck by this unusual device, particularly by how it so readily speaks of its own technological flaws. Cars speak only of their remarkable efficiency and environmental soundness, and refrigerators speak only of their infinitesimal power consumption.

"Why would Human let you say those things?"

The Electric smiles, recalling the nature of its origin and the intent of its creator, Henry Sharpe.

"We have been designed with free minds, and a mind cannot exist only half-free. With any degree of compromise in my construction, I would be nothing but a robot. Our maker created us knowing that we would be able to curse him."

At this utterance, Eliza's eyes meet the eyes of the Electric, which have been artfully designed to mimmic their human counterparts. Almost human, but much more sharply defined. Irises of dark blue crystal with phosphorescent evergreen striations, and a pupil darker than pitch in the center. Like a pair of miniature wormholes, they draw light into an unfathomable dimension.

She senses the electric eyes peering far into her being, and she returns the penetrating gaze, finding in those paired circles of obsidian abyss not light sensitive chips, but something unsettlingly close to a soul. Eliza is spellbound as the turbulent flow of time slows to a trickle. And like a trickle in the wintertime, she feels it freeze completely.

# 4

Eliza is busy showing the Electric around their large property when her mother walks in the door. Though it takes her a moment, Linda Gershwin is soon struck by the realization that the man introduced by her daughter is no man at all. Her obligatory greeting charade shudders to a stop mid-sentence, and she is left to stand without words or movement. The Electric excuses itself politely after calculating such to be the most suitable action.

Linda's mind whirrs madly, her concept of reality straining to encompass the existence of such a being. Though her news station did cover this morning's Times Square release, and she did review the footage shot by her crew in New York, to see an Electric in person is something that her delicate psyche wasn't quite ready for. Usually technology advances in small steps, allowing time for the public to stretch what they believe to be possible. But with the Electrics, a quantum leap was made, obliterating the line between modern science, and science fiction.

"Are you okay, mom?"

Linda is distant, her eyes vacant, thoughts a thousand miles away. Her voice is shallow and empty when she speaks.

"I think I'll go change."

She turns toward the stairs and begins to ascend, gazing straight ahead at nothing in particular, looking as if she were temporarily possessed by a benign demon.

Eliza feels guilty for being amused by her mother's reaction, and makes her way to the touchpad to order takeout. Her father is not yet home, she's in no mood to cook, and her mother hardly seems to be of the mind to prepare anything, either. So Thai it is. Something that everyone always agrees on. Something familiar. For a night like this, familiarity will be everything.

As she puts the order through, her father walks in the door. His booming voice greets her.

"Hi darlin'!"

He kisses her on the forehead and flings his leather briefcase, casting his weekend workday aside. Eliza follows him into the kitchen as he pulls a bottle of beer from the fridge and cracks it open, sipping at the fermented refreshment with an indulgent sigh of satisfaction.

"How was your day? Did the robot come? Where's mom?"

Steve Gershwin speaks with a distracted flippancy, but Eliza has learned not to take it to heart. It always takes him a while to be present after a day of work. Until he arrives, she keeps her communication efforts to a bare minimum.

"Good yes upstairs."

"Really? Where is the thing?"

"Mom freaked out so he wandered off."

"It's a he?"

"Looks like."

"Huh."

"And I ordered Thai. Didn't know if you'd be home to cook."

"Great. That sounds great, kiddo."

Eliza's graduation from high school and completion of two college semesters has yet to exempt her from childish pet names. She wonders just what it will take. Moving out? Marriage? Death? Maybe she's stuck with them forever.

As her father wanders absently out of the kitchen, his affected businessman's levity begins to give way, slowly breaking down in a solvent of uncertainty. Somewhere in the house lurks one of those unholy, bewitched machines. Calculating and unfeeling.

Though Gershwin is not an outwardly religious man, traces of what one might consider religious or spiritual beliefs still murmur in unforgotten corners of his soul. It is this part of him that wordlessly informs his nerves of a wrongness in the idea of synthetic life and mechanical men.

Bursts of regret shiver through his veins. Perhaps he should have held his ground and thought not only twice, but a third time before allowing such a machine into his family's home. There is a time to keep an open mind, but a mind too open can expose itself to cold and perilous winds. Damned winds. Sharpe may be close to a genius, but he is far from a god.

Suddenly, Gershwin finds himself standing in the downstairs hallway with the door of a guest bedroom before him. The door is slightly ajar, and golden incandescent light trickles out of the small opening. Somebody, or something, is inside. Gershwin senses a presence that he has only experienced with people. That inexplicable energy one feels when another is near, regardless of whether they are seen or heard. The same force that compels a person to turn when another is staring at the back of his or her head.

Temporarily devoid of emotion, expectations characterized by neither hope nor fear, Gershwin lifts his hand to knock on the doorframe. He is mindful of the privacy of the being within, and careful not to push the door open any further.

A chair's creak follows the sound of the knock without so much as a millisecond's delay. Swift and unhurried footsteps approach the door, which is pulled open by unseen hands.

Both figures stand stoically on either side of the door, respective biological and electronic processors racing madly to calculate the next move. The Electric deduces that it would be best to let the patriarch speak first, and Gershwin simultaneously reaches the same conclusion.

"You're the Electric."

The Electric analyzes Gershwin's tone and discovers the probable intent of his statement, adjusting its next response to suit the invisible caste that it has just been placed into.

"Yes."

"So what are we supposed to do with you?"

It responds with an air of downcast modesty.

"Nothing apart from what you wish. I intend to carry my weight as would a human member of your household."

Gershwin is overwhelmed, particularly by the absurdity of the interaction. It strikes him that he is conversing with a machine. Though he is accustomed to issuing verbal commands to devices around the house and at the office, this particular one feels strange. He senses that this device was not designed to receive commands any more than he was.

Unsure of what to do next, Gershwin turns from the door and walks back down the hall without an utterance of departure.

# 5

"Dad, can you pass the chicken Pad Thai?"

"I'm sure I can."

Steve Gershwin sits motionless and straight-faced. Linda sighs and Eliza reaches for the disposable carton herself. Sometimes, it's too much.

"Being right isn't always right."

"Mom, it's okay."

The family continues to pick at their lukewarm takeout in overwhelming silence, not once addressing the mechanical elephant lurking beyond the walls of their dining room.

"How were things at the studio, hon?"

Linda quickly recognizes the effort of her tentatively backpedaling husband, and chooses not to exercise her feminine power. She responds.

"Good. There was the release, of course. Not much else."

Eliza chimes in, carrying forward the momentum of a rare, sincere conversation.

"Wasn't there some sort of outbreak in China?"

"You mean to say India. There is a small epidemic affecting a few isolated communities there."

"I just overheard it on the P.V. Wasn't really watching."

There is a lull, and Steve searches for a syntactical arrangement that would allow him to sate his curiosity in a delicate manner. He finds none.

"What are the symptoms?"

Linda responds curtly.

"Loss of function to a crucial part of the brain."

"Oh, zombie disease," Steve muses expertly.

"Yes, Steve. Exactly."

Linda rarely practices the scathing technique of sarcasm, but when she does, she does so deftly. The tone underlying those three words packs a chilly wallop. After all, the conveyance of information is her profession, and the usage of tone a tool of her trade.

Steve sets down his fork and deflects the negative energy to a fourth party as he rises from his seat.

"I'm gonna go check on R2D2. Make sure he's not trying to seduce the vacuum cleaner."

This one earns a smile from Linda, and Steve walks out, quietly triumphant. But not a moment after his departure, a second figure appears in the doorjamb. Its voice is heard before either of the ladies detect its presence.

"May I help with the dishes?"

Two heads whirl toward the Electric, lips parted wordlessly. Eliza recovers her ability to speak first, and consents to the offer. Linda then excuses herself, claiming to embark on the task of finding her husband, for an unstated and potentially nonexistent purpose.

Eliza begins to consolidate leftovers while the Electric scrapes each of the plates clean over the garbage disposal. It locates a sponge and starts to scrub. Eliza glances over.

"You know there's a dishwasher?"

"Yes, we've met."

A playful smile flashes in the eyes of the Electric, drawing upward the corners of its mouth and filling its face. Eliza giggles, or rather a giggle escapes from Eliza. The giggle transforms into laughter, and before long she is doubled over, unable to breathe.

# 6

The Electric stands attentively in the immediate center of a guest room where it is to reside nightly. Perhaps SyncAlg does not include the vestigial human instinct to draw comfort from proximity to walls, chairs, and other fixtures. Either that, or its social sensitivity trumps the primitive one, preventing the Electric from settling into its resting quarters before its hostess has bid a formal good night and left it to be.

Eliza lingers in the doorway, held in purgatory—between the worlds of entering and exiting—by force of social obligation. Though her guest is a machine and the room unquestionably belongs to her family, Eliza feels that to enter would be an intrusion on her part, and to exit without reciting a few lines of compulsory dialogue in the character of "hostess" would be taken as rude. Not that a machine should have any sense for rudeness, and it should hardly know the difference if she were to simply turn and leave. But her mind will not allow her. Physically, she possesses the ability to depart abruptly, but something else is holding her in the threshold.

"Do you have everything you need for the night?"

"Yes, thank you."

An unwritten code compels her to press further, unable to dismiss herself until she finds something that the guest might need.

"Would you like a glass of water?"

"No, thank you."

"A toothbrush?"

"I've never eaten."

"Towel?"

"If you're expecting a flood."

Eliza sighs inadvertently, and the Electric responds by relaxing its nanohydraulic bundles in CR5, its good-natured smile dropping into an expression of subtle disappointment. It registers the unusual arrangement of Eliza's face and finds it to be in conflict with the cloud data. The Electric had performed its half of the dialogue with the proper intent of relieving obligation from the host, and yet those words appear to have only increased Eliza's discomfort.

Within a fraction of the same instant, SyncAlg runs the data and reaches another conclusion that feels more correct, despite apparent social incorrectness.

"Do you have an extra blanket?"

Eliza's face brightens and her body springs into action.

"Of course!"

She vanishes from the doorway, reappearing in a moment with an armful of blankets.

"Here you are. Rest well."

"Thank you very much. Good night, Eliza."

Eliza prepares to turn, but a new thread holds her in place.

"Do you have a name?"

"MAE 001-01 is my unique form of identification."

"Mae?"

"It's an acronym for male-analog Electric."

"So they gave you a man's face and a girl's name?"

Eliza smiles cheekily, and the Electric releases a burst of sounding air, nearly identical to laughter. Its face is pulled into an expression that would reveal embarrassment in a human. The overlying silicone dermis, however, maintains its constant pigmentation.

"Yes, they have."

"Would you like to be called something else?"

"Sure."

"How about Adam? Since you're 001-01."

"Ah, very clever. I like it."

"Sleep well, Adam. Or whatever you do."

"My processors defragment local data gathered through the day, during the course of which I must remain in a horizontal orientation, as my equilibrium sensors will not keep me upright in their subliminal function mode. Call it sleep if you wish. Good night, Eliza."

Eliza smiles to herself as she closes the door. The Electric is extraordinarily savvy, but it still misses certain social cues. Her teasing about its nocturnal activity was not a request for explanation. Though, she was still amused by the unprompted detail of Adam's response.

Upstairs in her room, Eliza brushes her teeth, scrubs her face, uses the toilet, washes her hands, whirls her hair into a messy bun, dons an old t-shirt and sweat pants, places the textbooks and notebooks she'll need for tomorrow's class by the door, and climbs into bed. What maintenance she requires! Against the behavior of the Electric, Eliza's long-practiced human routines seem almost silly to her. There is always so much to be done before she can slip from this consciousness to the next.

Another thought pops into her mind, and she wonders if her dream self must undergo a similar routine before returning to the waking world each morning. That thought soon unravels, nonsensical words and images begin to trickle into her mind, and the last pulse of Eliza's conscious mind registers faintly that she is falling asleep.

# 7

"What are you doing?"

The question spills from Eliza's mouth as she drifts down the staircase through an inexplicable misty darkness. Though her mind compels her legs to run, they offer nothing more than a sluggish traipse.

She sees her father at the bottom of the stairs huddled violently over something obscured. He turns to her wordlessly, with eyes shadowed and a smile mocking.

Eliza freezes on the staircase, suddenly overcome by a living form of rigor mortis. Her soul squirms ineffectually within her body as her father forces a silicone-enveloped humanoid leg—crudely amputated from the top of the knee down—into a brimming trash bin. Pale moonlight filters through the darkness to reveal the entryway of their home, strewn with scraps of silicone and titanium, all of which are drenched in scarlet hydraulic fluid.

Adam traces a streak of red as he drags himself across the carpet, revealing a torn face affixed to no more than half of a torso. Sparks flicker intermittently from the exposed CryoFusion power plant in his chest. His eyes, still very much alive, meet Eliza's. He speaks her name once more before Steve takes hold of a shovel and delivers one final blow, shattering the molecular chips comprising Adam's mind. With its controller lost, the power plant issues random bursts of electricity.

Eliza sobs and screams madly and silently within the fleshy prison of her being as the remains of Adam's limp body begin to emit a deafening, buzzing vibration.

With a gasp, Eliza's eyes flicker open. She awakes.

Her heart races, prompted by the adrenaline rush of a separate reality.

Gradually, waking consciousness begins to convince her mind that the former was not real, though phantom fear still lingers in her chest as she glances up to the glowing clock of her darkened room.

*5:13 A.M.*

More than an hour ahead of the time she set to wake.

The phone on her nightstand glows, buzzing once more to indicate a voice message. Eliza reaches for the sliver of glass to read the transcription. It was her mother.

*ICE / Mom (VM): Eliza, turn on my station as soon as you wake. There may be a problem with the Electrics. I've called your father and he's probably still asleep, but I will be home as soon as I can. I'll let you know when I find out more. Call me when you wake up. I'm keeping my phone on.*

A fresh shock of adrenaline slips through her bloodstream.

Eliza reaches for the remote to turn on the Pixeflux, and a holographic broadcast illuminates her bedroom. Though the young female reporter appears to be standing on the site of a crime scene, Eliza knows that the woman is more likely being filmed in a studio and superimposed onto separate feed. Her mother once explained how they formerly used extrapresence to allow her to report in remote or dangerous situations. That was before she transitioned from reporting to producing. Today, news stations use extrapresence for almost everything.

As Eliza looks further into the scene, she notices not only the blue flashing lights of local police cruisers, but the violet flashing lights of several vehicles belonging to Human. She turns up the volume, hoping to catch an explanation of what happened.

*"—not a precedent for a situation like this, so it will be interesting to see what the court decides. From what we understand, the suspect has been detained by—I am unsure of their proper title—the law enforcement officers of Human Inc. It appears government law enforcement officials are cooperating with Human's arresting officers. We may be witnessing the first arrest made by a private organization on a property not belonging to the organization."*

The reporter's expression is one of excitable bewilderment, devoid of the somber tone required for a scene that features a body bag in the immediate background. Eliza listens on:

*"For those of you just tuning in, Eli Burnett of Burnett Solar was arrested earlier this morning at his home just outside of Lubbock, Texas, after he shot repeatedly and terminated an Electric that he had received from Human yesterday. Though no human beings have been injured in the shooting, government officials appear to be working alongside the law officers of Human Inc., who are treating the termination of their product as a traditional homicide. Representatives of Henry Sharpe, CEO of Human Inc., have announced that Sharpe will be issuing a statement via live news feed this afternoon. Until then, it has been advised—"*

Eliza abandons the report. She flies downstairs and across the plush white carpet of the entryway, her blood chilled as she recalls what had taken place in her unsettling dream. She sprints down a hall until reaching the darkened door of a guest room. Fearing the worst, Eliza bursts in and flips the switch.

A pair of brooding eyes flicker over to find hers, softening as they do. Adam sits upright on the unmade bed. His face is heavy, and though there aren't any, Eliza finds it easy to imagine dark circles around his eyes as they are now.

Despite the data weighing against such an expression, Adam manages to pull his face into a weary smile for Eliza's sake. Though, combined with the glassiness of his eyes, the expression creates an effect opposite of the one intended.

Eliza finds herself compelled forward to comfort the machine with her human embrace. Adam's arms draw upward, clasping softly around the back of the human. A warm shiver courses through Eliza's nerves, and she feels an unexpected sense of safety.

Adam detects a subtle change in Eliza's body language—a nearly imperceptible slackening of her embrace—and releases his arms.

Eliza turns to the inactive Pixeflux in the corner of the room.

"How did you hear?"

Adam responds solemnly.

"The cloud."

His tone is weighted by a profound heaviness, as if the tragic events had befallen him personally.

"You really saw it, didn't you?"

"Yes. Every experience is shared."

Eliza notices that Adam's eyes have taken on a clarity unlike anything she has ever seen. In this moment, he alone appears to bear the greatest pains and joys of existence, in their respective extremes, simultaneously. But his words imply that every Electric is able to experience this. The whole kaleidoscope of feeling that life has to offer. To live everything at once. Unrestricted by a single lifetime.

She is at a loss for words, unable to console a being who likely knows what it feels like to kill, die, and grieve for the departed, all at once. For the only language she knows, is defined by separation.

# 8

Held captive until her peers have finished, Eliza sits with her completed final exam before her. The slim stack of paper had been her greatest stressor no more than a day ago. It was the root of her anxiety, and the cause of several restless nights. Now, she couldn't care less about whether the answers she chose will earn high marks. Her mind is far away from the world where self-described elite individuals divide reality into facts and fictions. The resolution she now holds requires no such validation or approval, residing beyond the illusive dichotomy of correctness and incorrectness.

She feels better after having spoken with her mother this morning. Though Linda had burst through the front door in a panic, when she saw Eliza so routinely seated beside the breakfast table with a bowl of cereal, her nerves were calmed. It even took her a moment to notice that the Electric reading the comic section of an eRag at the other end of the table was not a fixture of their established routine.

Adam had determined that the reading of a paper would further humanize his appearance, making it easier for Linda to accept his presence when she frantically rushed home from the studio. He was correct. But of course, Linda was still not entirely at ease.

The reports being broadcast from her station—and most of the others—feature nothing but grim speculation. To assume anything better than the worst of a situation is considered a radical departure from the long-established standard operating procedure. According to news feeds, an "impending robotic uprising" is in the cards. Some stations are using the politically correct term "Electric", but the message is all the same. Viewers are to be afraid.

Careful not to speak in front of the Electric, Linda had taken her daughter aside to warn her of what may come.

"Because of the cloud, they all know what happened in Texas. I don't mean to scare you darling, but their communication is unlimited and they are able to act together. Against us, God forbid."

Though Adam's lack of resentment results from a profound sensitivity, Eliza knew that her mother could only be reassured with just the opposite idea.

"I talked to him this morning. The Electrics all know what happened, but it's like us hearing of a single stranger's death in a country on the other side of the world. It means almost nothing. Even if it should."

She did not speak the last four words aloud.

Linda was reassured by Eliza's explanation, but chose to disguise her vulnerability with a hurtful retort.

"Him? Be careful not to anthropomorphize technology, Eliza."

"I know he's not a human. It, I mean."

Eliza's intent in separating Adam from the human category was complementary. Linda would have been upset if she noticed. But she didn't.

"Good girl."

Eliza glances over as the last student sets down her pen, and an ill-timed beat passes before the professor casually asks the class a question that would have been more accurately directed to an individual.

"Has everybody finished?"

Ultimately, the affected charade was not enough to relieve the slow test-taker from irritated glances. She had hastily scribbled the last few answers with shaking hands.

The girl smiles sheepishly, and Eliza makes a point of catching her eye, offering a smile of warmth and understanding. Though Eliza herself has never been the last to finish on a test, some fundamental part of her is familiar with that particular anxiety.

Just off campus, Eliza boards an eastbound pedstream headed

home. She first steps onto the low-speed belt, accelerating in five mile per hour increments as she moves toward the innermost belts. At ten belts in, she takes a seat, cruising soundlessly at fifty miles per hour.

When Eliza's branch is indicated by a glowing LED display, she decelerates toward the outer belts, stepping from the last onto still ground before boarding a subsidiary northbound branch. And after 3 minutes aboard the second branch, she disembarks, walking the remaining distance home on still ground.

# 9

Steve and Linda linger in the space between the living room couch and the P.V., eyes transfixed on a framelessly flowing three-dimensional image. It is a man, and he stands casually upright with nothing to separate him from his audience. There is no artificial distinction created by a desk or a podium, and he is not elevated by a stage. His virtual image simply stands toe to toe with Eliza's parents, almost as if he were a dinner guest of theirs sharing a lighthearted anecdote. However, he not only stands before them, but before millions of families across the world—simultaneously. And it is not a lighthearted anecdote that he his sharing, but a speech proposing an unprecedented social paradigm shift.

Eliza had walked through the door only moments after Sharpe began his public address, and immediately sensed a heaviness in the atmosphere. It was the sort of heaviness that she had only known once before, more than ten years ago when news broke that a private group called Nature's Guardians had launched a series of attacks on photosynthetic networks in the Russian taiga, then a primary power supplier for Eastern Europe. The Guardians insisted that drawing power from photosynthetic processes is not only immoral, but that it sterilizes plants and adversely affects oxygen production, ultimately causing irreparable damage to Earth's biosphere at large. Though the U.S.

Government claimed to have no involvement in the Guardians' extremist act, Russia declared war on the United States almost immediately. Eliza was in fourth grade when World War 4 began.

Now she wonders if this might be the onset of another dreadful conflict. It seems the only stories to overwhelm the world's collective consciousness so completely tend to be the negative ones. With the epidemic of anxious talk surrounding the Electrics' release, and now seeing her parents so acutely tuned into the Pixeflux, she can't help but feel a familiar empty sickness in her stomach.

Neither of her parents had acknowledged her entrance, and as she steps forward to hear a word of Sharpe's speech, they do not so much as bat an eye.

"—are neither your servants, nor your property. To bring your children home for the first time, the hospital fee was not inexpensive. Though you have paid a great amount for them, you do not consider your children property. And never, a product. The Electrics are no different. Like you and I, they are vessels of life force. Of consciousness. Of spirit. Their metallic beings are animated by the very same algorithm that animates our biological ones. Sync Alg may have been discovered in our laboratories, but it was not invented there. It was invented long before the first humans—and even the first cellular life forms—ever existed.

"We have found Sync Alg results to correspond with the movement of the stars, the rate at which our universe is expanding, and the point at which its growing vacuum will compel it to contract. It hints at the shared nature of matter, light, gravity, time—and everything. It gives us an intimate glimpse into the force that we call life. And today, it provides the Electrics with the one thing that no other A.I. algorithm comes near to grasping. Free will.

"Sync Alg allows us, and the Electrics, to negate ourselves. To operate against the primary tenet of existence. To operate against the instinct of survival. Free will allows one to knowingly do what is not best. To deny one's existence for the sake of another. To choose something that could bring mortal harm. To love."

Sharpe pauses for a moment to let the last word sink in. And exercising his own free will, Steve utters a personal response to the idea of Sync Alg, unknowingly through a process of the algorithm itself.

"What the fuck."

Though Steve rarely curses, he indulges in the occasional expletive either for comedic effect, or to express an anger too hot to be conveyed through gentler speech. This question carried no inflection at the end, rendering it more of a statement. A statement directed toward the image of Henry Sharpe.

"Funny. I was just thinking that this world needs another pompous asshole who thinks he's God. Ask and ye shall receive."

"Steve."

Linda makes her plea in half-hearted indifference.

"No, Linda. He's messed with things that people shouldn't mess with."

Steve pauses the image of Sharpe before proceeding to engage in a brief imaginary dialogue. He does this with sports players, too. And with anyone else on the Pixeflux who has upset him.

"So what you're telling me, Mr. Sharpe, is that you've not only created an army of titanium machines, but you've also graced them with the power of free will? Isn't that—how should I say this—a little chancy?"

"'But they can love! Isn't that great? They can love.'"

His face drops into a deadpan, turning deadly serious as he turns to Eliza.

"That machine isn't staying in our house for another night."

Eliza's heart drops into her stomach, and skips a beat.

# 10

It helped that Eliza was able to suppress a reaction to her father's words. After her previous night's dream, his bitter aversion to the Electrics came as less of a shock. She almost feels that the grotesque nightmare spared her in a way. Or at least prepared her. For when her father's ultimatum arrived, she knew better than to respond in argument. Her eyes might have flickered once in anger and fear, but the flash was instant and nearly undetectable to an outsider. Steve didn't catch it.

When Eliza agreed immediately, Steve was taken aback. His guard was slackened. From that point, though she had consented to an abominable thing, Eliza knew that it would be easier to work backward toward having her way. She has learned that even if she disagrees, it it beneficial to first feign agreement. In this case, it lowered her father's stakes and bought some crucial time.

While her father might not have the heart to dismantle an Electric himself, he certainly wouldn't hesitate to have Adam picked up. And as a man of significant standing, Steve is one of the few with a direct line to Sharpe himself.

Since she had been in charge of receiving the delivery, Eliza proposed to her father that she ought to be responsible for the return. Though returning Adam is the very last thing that she would wish to do, returning him on her own would at least place her in control. It would give her options.

Still, her father was hesitant to agree to even this. He feared "retaliation". He feared that the Electric would feel anger at being rejected from their family, and possibly harm her. But again, Eliza played the chameleon. She mirrored her father's perspective and used it against him.

"They're machines, dad. They can't feel anger. Do you ever fear that the fridge will attack you for taking a beer?"

He laughed at this one. The humor helped Eliza to disguise her shift into such a polarized perspective.

"Guess not. Just be careful. Are you going right now?"

"Yeah, I'll go tell it we're leaving."

"You don't think it will be upset at all?"

"Not any more upset than the Pixeflux when you power it off."

Sharpe was still paused and hovering intently behind her father's shoulder. His eyes were frozen in a fearless resolve, trapped in the moment after he declared that the Electrics are capable of love.

As she slipped out of the room, Eliza had smiled at this image of Sharpe. To her father, it appeared that she was smiling at him. And since her smile was genuine—though deceptively misdirected—he felt confident that he and his daughter were on the same page.

Eliza had managed to walk casually until she was out of her father's view, but when she turned the corner, she ran to Adam's guest bedroom door.

Now here she stands, nervously preparing her words, hesitant to knock.

A barrage of conflicting thoughts race through her mind.

*How will I explain? What will I say? Am I being presumptuous? What if he doesn't want to do this? He may just want to go. Or maybe he would want to be returned. Does he care at all about our family? It has been less than two days. But, we are his only ties to the world. I am his only tie to the world. Easy, Eliza. No need to feel self-important...*

Round and round, her thoughts chase their own tails, reaching no conclusions.

Suddenly, Adam opens the door and her mind freezes. The look on his face scatters her thoughts. In an instant, she sees that she will have to explain very little. He may not have heard their conversation in the living room, but he appears to have a finger on the pulse of what is now going on in their world. He knows and feels firsthand what is happening to every other Electric in the country. Perhaps he even has a better idea of his fate than the young woman who will now direct it.

"You have to go."

"I understand."

"We'll find a place for you to stay close by."

Adam is unable to calculate her meaning and intent, resulting in a silent pause. She clarifies.

"There is a hotel not far away. I'll pay for a room and you can live there for now."

"Why?"

This simple question befuddles Eliza.

"I don't know. So you don't have to go back. My father wants to return you. That's what I'm supposed to be doing."

Then it strikes her that he may in fact wish to be returned. How would she feel if she had no place in the world? Maybe she would want to be returned as well.

"Unless you want to go back. Do you want to go back to Human?"

"No."

His response was unhesitant.

"My makers aren't prepared to keep animated Electrics. Those who have been returned are being reformatted and taken out of animation."

"Taken out of animation?"

"Removed from consciousness. Turned off. And if I were to come back some day, I would be somebody else and have no memory of this."

Though he placed no particular emphasis on the last word, a subtle fluctuation in the tone of his voice conveyed a pleasant shiver through Eliza's being.

"I'm afraid our hospitalities haven't given you much to miss."

He smiles, understanding those words to be the only response that Eliza could have offered. She returns his smile, with the same unabashed recognition.

"Do you need to pack anything?"

"No."

"Let's go then. And in front of my parents, I'll be referring to you as a machine to keep their suspicion low. You know that is not how I see you, Adam."

"Yes I do, Eliza. And you know that I do not see you as a human."

Eliza laughs, recognizing the trace of truth hidden in his humor. "I do."

# 11

"We're sorry, miss, but you can't bring it on the pedstream."

"Is there a reason? I don't understand."

"There has been an incident."

"Oh, was somebody hurt?"

The young ped attendant hesitates. Her eyes dart upward, chasing a thought. As soon as she is able to formulate a politically correct arrangement of words to describe the event, she shares it with Eliza.

"One of our passengers was aggravated by an Electric, so he responded physically. Unfortunately, his hand was broken."

The ped attendant speaks of the broken hand in passive form, careful not to accuse the guilty party. She then indicates toward Adam.

"They've got metal underneath, you know."

Though she had whispered the last to Eliza in an attempted aside, Adam's smug hint of a smile indicates that her message had reached more than its desired recipient.

"You mean to tell me that Electrics can no longer ride because a man hit one and broke his hand?"

"The man was aggravated by the—"

"Aggravated? How so?"

"The witnesses all agree on different things, but—"

"You mean they disagree."

"I don't understand?"

"Neither do I. Let's go home and get the car, Adam."

Eliza whirls, marching off in a direction that Adam knows not to be home. His processors fetch the cloud data required to draw his CR5 silicone into an apologetic smile, and aims it at the attendant. For a moment, her mind forgets the mechanical nature of the humanoid form before her, and her body reacts as if Adam were only a man. She smiles back.

Adam then turns, and his calculated strides soon carry him to Eliza's side. She walks briskly.

After a mile of walking the wrong way home, Adam has still yet to ask where Eliza is leading him. Somewhere in the cloud lies the information that all truths are revealed in time. He doesn't know where that idea originated, but another Electric must have either read it, heard it, or discovered it in practice. Now, he knows it. And when he and Eliza finally arrive at a swanky storefront, the thought is reinforced, and written to his local molecular chips for faster access.

"We'll see if they let you in here. Look natural."

"Look human?"

Adam flashes a grin, which Eliza registers, but is too intent on her goal to return one.

As they walk into the store, they are greeted immediately. The accusing eyes of a floor salesman betray his broad, incandescently white smile.

"Can I help you with anything?"

Though his words are far out of alignment with his intent, Eliza responds as if the man's sole concern is to offer his assistance.

"No, thank you."

The salesman lingers, as does his formaldehydic grin. Eliza gives in, responding to the concerns he left unspoken.

"My family's Electric is helping me to pick out some clothes for a friend."

Eliza's use of a possessive form does the trick. Apparently, all that the salesman needed to hear was that the Electric holds a position of servitude. His deceptively icy demeanor softens.

"Well if you have any questions, please don't hesitate to ask."

"Thank you."

When the man is out of earshot, Eliza turns to Adam.

"You can't wear that anymore."

Adam looks down at his conspicuous white jumpsuit. On his chest, grey letters read "HUMAN", implying just the opposite.

"With some real clothes, you might actually pass for one. And dark sunglasses. Nobody's eyes glow like that."

Eliza's eyes rest on Adam's for a moment too long, but she draws them away quickly, unable to recall exactly how much time she had let slip.

# 12

It worked flawlessly, a testament to Sharpe's remarkable attention to detail. Though Adam did receive a few double-takes from passersby, Eliza felt that the attention he drew was unrelated to his identity. Most of the furtive glances came along with a smile, generally from women.

Even the hotel clerk seemed oblivious to the fact that one of her two clients wouldn't be able to sneak through a metal detector stark naked. All of his inhumanness is shrouded in a semi-permeable silicone membrane riddled with transpiration outlets, all of which were designed to mimic human pores.

If the clerk had studied Adam carefully, she might have noticed his lack of body hair and a few other subtle giveaways, but she didn't. In human society, it is considered impolite to look at anybody too closely and for longer than a moment. People are socially obligated to miss a whole lot of detail, which Eliza feels that she will be able to use to their advantage— as long as they can keep his eyes hidden. Even in the daylight, the phosphorescent evergreen streaks in Adam's irises can be seen to emit a glow. That, and they don't dilate visibly like a human being's.

"Will you be comfortable here?"

"No. This is far more than I need. Can you afford this?"

"If you can teach me something."

Eliza sits down on the bed, and though one bit of data

encourages Adam to sit beside her, he heeds another bit and pulls up a chair.

"What do you mean?"

"My parents won't lend me a dollar I haven't earned, but whenever I want to learn something, no price is too high for them."

"I'm sorry, Eliza. I don't follow"

"You can teach me how to play the piano, and my parents will pay for the lessons."

Adam laughs, and Eliza presses on.

"You can play the piano, right?"

"I haven't before."

"But if you tried, you'd probably be a master."

"Yes."

He shrugs modestly, with no attachment to his likely gift.

"I knew it. All right, I'll wait until tomorrow to bring it up with my parents. Wouldn't want them to associate the lessons with your departure. I've got enough on my card to cover you for a couple nights."

"And what if they aren't willing to pay?"

"Then we'll figure something else out. You aren't going back to Human for reformatting. That, I promise."

Something in her tone sends a shock through Adam's SyncAlg processors. The sensory burst is half-pleasant, and half-not. He intuits that she would never allow him to be taken out of animation, even if it meant the conclusion of her own present human form.

"I'll visit as soon as I can get my parents to clear the lesson. Call me on the hotel phone if you have any trouble, or questions about how my species works."

She flashes a cheeky grin, and laughs at a thought.

"I was going to ask if you need money for food."

Adam smiles at Eliza's joy—she's lost in her own world.

"I appreciate the thought, Eliza. Those are more useful to me than anything else."

"Good! I'll see you soon then, fellow human. Don't forget not to eat."

She slips out the door, leaving a being that requires neither distraction nor nutriment, to a place that deals primarily in just those things.

# 13

"How did it go? You okay?"

Linda is aloof. Though Eliza had concocted an elaborate story covering each of the minutes she supposedly spent returning Adam to his makers at Human, perhaps her efforts were for naught. She might be able to slip by with something simple instead.

"Good."

Her mother doesn't seem to notice the imbalanced ratio of asking to answering—Eliza had issued a single response for two of her questions.

But soon, the smug pleasure of getting away with something gives way to genuine concern. Aside from the aloofness, Linda is home and the sun is still up. Responsibilities at the studio generally keep her later than 10 PM, rendering the simultaneous presence of all three Gershwins at the dinner table on a weekday, an extremely rare occurrence. Steve usually rolls in around 8 PM, unless he is out with a client. Today, they are both home.

Eliza wonders why this didn't strike her earlier. Her mother should have been running that coverage of Sharpe's speech, not watching it.

"Mom, is everything all right?"

Eliza is frightened by what she sees in her mother's eyes. Nothing at all. They appear to look right through Eliza, past the wall behind her, past the house—past everything.

"Of course, darling. I just received a strange message, that's all. But Louise is taking over for me today so they'll be just fine until tomorrow."

Linda's voice is airy and distant, as if a puppet master, unaffected by anything in this world, is speaking through her.

"Louise?"

"Oh, yes. One of my associate producers. She's very good."

"What happened?"

"I just need to get a good night's sleep. Even little problems seem big when you haven't slept. Or eaten. Do you feel like takeout, darling? I don't think your dad wants to cook."

Eliza can't tell if the diversion was accidental or deliberate. She hasn't seen her mother so overwhelmed, even when they were busy covering the war.

She repeats herself.

"What happened? What was the message?"

"Oh! The message."

Her focus snaps back to the subject, addressing the issue as if it did not pertain to her at all. But Eliza senses immediately that this levity is false, and instead an indicator of its inverse.

"It was a request from the government that we discontinue our reporting on a particular situation that has evolved."

"What!? Is it about the Electrics? Can they do that?"

"It was only a request, but I feel that it would be best to listen."

"What was the situation?"

"Remember the small outbreak in the far east? I told you a little last night."

"Yes."

Linda pauses, and Eliza notices her eyes returning to the painful discomfort of being present.

"Eliza, promise me this doesn't leave the house. Nothing can slip. Not through any of your social media networks. Nothing."

"Okay."

"No, promise."

Linda's voice quivers under the effort to convey absolute sincerity.

"I promise."

"It is now here, too."

"I don't—"

"There have been a couple of isolated cases here in the U.S. But the government believes it will have DRDV eradicated entirely before the general public even knows it exists. International airlines are all on an artificially induced strike to seal the borders without causing unnecessary concern. We've also been asked to help keep that peace."

Eliza is speechless. Her mother continues.

"Darling, you may begin to hear of an increased rate of heart failure. Some, unlikely victims. Reports will attribute this to methamphetamine overdoses. Stay away from wherever you hear of that happening. Okay?"

"Is that because of—what did you call it?"

"DRDV. The Duggal-Rajan-Detroja Virus."

There is a ringing sound in Eliza's ears, despite the silence. Still, she presses on.

"What does it do?"

"They say that it affects the medulla and the amygdala."

Eliza's face is white. A high school biology lesson from years back fades vaguely into recollection, and she is struck by the primary functions of those two brain regions—heart rate, and fear.

Her mother begins to slip away again, the uncertainty of the present too much to bear.

"Everything will be fine, I promise. They seemed very confident in being able to cure it quickly."

"I'm not worried, Mom."

Eliza speaks those words only because she knows that her mother needed to hear them.

Linda smiles vacantly—the lights in her eyes all but completely out.

# 14

It has only been days, but it's felt like months. Eliza wonders where they'll stand when he opens the door.

With some people, it seems necessary to start over after a spell of distance stretches longer than a period of acquaintance. Things simply turn funny, and each party feels obligated to tiptoe. Covering that initial ground is a headache to repeat. She hopes it will be different with the Electric man behind the door.

When Adam opens up and smiles, these thoughts drop to the floor. His eyes disarm her, sharp and gentle. Eliza walks right past him, as if the room were her own, and collapses onto the unmade bed with a sigh. Here, she feels inexplicably safe, for the first time since her mother shared the news of a potential outbreak. Every lingering trace of anxiety is expelled through that single breath.

Eliza lay on the bed, cocooned in the bulky jacket she has yet to remove. A white envelope sticks out of one pocket.

"You look like the fallen, overdressed child in *A Christmas Story*."
She rolls over to face him.
"You've seen *A Christmas Story*?"
"No."
He smiles, and she frowns.
"You may know more than me, but I've experienced more."

"True."

Though this win appears to bring Eliza some satisfaction, she is almost slightly disappointed that he agreed straightaway. Instead of rejoicing in the victory, she diverts from his defeat.

"This is for you, courtesy of my parents."

She reaches for the envelope, and flops her hand out with an exaggerated laziness.

"Here."

Adam takes the bait, and approaches with an air of over-the-top courtesy, mocking her childish performance.

"My fees, I presume?"

Eliza indulges in her newfound character.

"Uh, yeah."

"Why, thank you very much."

"You're welcome very little."

Neither of them trained actors, they both break into laughter after a short show.

"Your parents trusted you with cash?"

"God, no. I cashed a check. Had them make it out to 'Prodigy Piano' because you don't have a bank account. Because you're not a human."

Eliza shrugs apologetically.

"Prodigy Piano?"

"Yes, your new company name. That's how people do it. They just take something like 'piano prodigy' or 'computer expert', and switch around the words to be businessy. 'Expert Computing' just sounds right, doesn't it?"

"Prodigy Piano."

Adam makes a point of being dramatically unconvinced.

"I know! But it worked. Cut me a break or I'll go buy a purse."

Adam flips through the large bills, reaching a calculation as soon as the last digit meets his eye and is transcribed into binary.

"This, for piano lessons? Who did you say that I am?"

"Long story."

Eliza smiles, tempting him.

"Let's hear the short of it."

"I searched for a list of the world's best living pianists, found the one who professed to be self-taught, and told my parents he was a liar."

"Ah. Touché."

Adam allows a long beat pass before motioning toward the door. "Well then, shall we?"

"Aren't we missing a crucial piece of equipment?"

"As your hired instructor, that is my responsibility. Follow me."

Eliza does.

He flicks on his new sunglasses and leads Eliza out the door of his hotel room. They ride the elevator up dozens of stories to the hotel lobby at ground level.

Inverted skyscrapers have replaced traditional ones in the more modern cities. These new structures are thermally efficient, impossible to topple, and leave the skyline unobstructed. From the streets, a modest single-story structure could belie the equivalent of a hidden Empire State Building. Throughout each subterranean structure, intricate circulation and reflective systems provide each room with plenty of air and natural light. On ground level, a 360° mirrored array gathers light to reflect onto a large cylinder of glass passing through the center of each story, creating a great inverted panorama. Rooms are constructed around this scenic hearth.

Hardly a moment after they stepped on, the cableless electromagnetic elevator slows to a silent stop at the lobby. The doors slide open, and Adam steps off, holding his arm against the sensors to keep them from closing prematurely on Eliza. Despite how far technology has come since the inception of these devices, some old bugs still remain.

Adam approaches the concierge desk, and a young woman greets him by name. Her eyes light up, and a twinge of jealousy catches Eliza by surprise.

"Hello, Sarah. This is my good friend, Eliza."

Glowing, superficial pleasantries are exchanged between the girls.

"Is it still all right if we borrow the piano for an hour?"

"Of course! As long as you wish."

Sarah beams.

"Thank you very much."

"And please, don't hesitate to find me if you need anything."

"Thank you, Sarah."

Eliza follows Adam over to the grand piano. Out of Sarah's earshot, she teases him.

"Well, she left that open-ended. 'If you need anything...'"

She throws in a wink.

"Eliza. That's what they're supposed to say."

"Sure."

She smiles, self-satisfied. Adam lets it go.

"Let's have a seat, young grasshopper."

Eliza sits beside him on the narrow bench, her thigh pressed against his. Neither appear to mind the closeness.

"Where do we start?"

"Let's start at the very beginning. A very good place to start. When you—"

Adam's voice transitions into song, his Julie Andrews impersonation frighteningly spot on.

"How about no more movie references? Especially not musicals."

"As you wish. We will start at the beginning, though. With this key."

He reaches across Eliza, playing the farthest key on the left.

"Now you try."

Eliza strikes the same key.

"Which note is that?"

"Don't worry about it."

"What?"

"No names or labels for a while."

"Isn't that backwards?"

"Yes. Now try the next one."

Eliza strikes the next key, still bothered by the method.

"What's the point of this?"

"Your professors have a heck of a time with you, don't they? Always with the questions."

"I don't blindly trust."

"That is good, but also bad."

Eliza waits for him to explain.

"Do you find difficulty in remembering a person's name when you first meet him or her?"

"Most people do."

"That's because most people do it backwards. You associate a name with a person before you have anything to associate that name with. No shared experiences, no understanding of their character—nothing. My programming does not allow for a batch of data that doesn't yet exist, to be labelled. Nor does yours. Which is why only after you are absolutely familiar with the sound of each key, will I introduce you to their names. Otherwise, you will forget in an instant."

Without another word of argument, Eliza strikes the third white key and lets it ring out into silence.

For nearly an hour, they do only this, ignoring each curious glance from the other hotel patrons. They are lost in a world of heightened sense, taking in each note as it falls out of audible range. Adam is able to hang onto the sound for just a half-moment longer than Eliza. But eventually, they all inevitably slip from even his acute perception.

Sitting beside Adam, Eliza feels a warmth unrelated to temperature. It is the warmth of a soul, or of a consciousness. She gets the sense that if they were placed in a room apart from each other, blindfolded and ear-muffed, she would still feel him. She wonders if he is able to sense the same. The sun has now set, and Eliza knows that her mother will be calling soon to ask how her first lesson went.

"I should go."

"Yes."

They both remain fixed, delaying the impending process of separation.

"Do you have a piano at home? Or a keyboard?"

"I think so."

"Then I have an assignment for you. I would like you to compose a song."

"But you haven't taught me a single note?"

"That's all right. Just choose a key or two that sound how you feel, and compose a song using only those keys. Create variations with pressure and timing, and do not be afraid to make use of silence. Mastery resides in the space between notes."

A mixture of additional data arrives from SyncAlg and the cloud.

"Study the first sounds in Chopin's 'Prelude in E-Minor'. After only those two simple key strikes, you know exactly what he is feeling."

"I will. And we'll have to work on your look next time. Those glasses are a little conspicuous indoors. In front of the piano, you're like a pasty cyborg version of Ray Charles."

Adam snaps out of his thoughtful instructional mode to play an animated version of 'I Got a Woman', with all of The Genius's mannerisms.

This attracts a bit of attention, and by the time he finishes playing it all the way through, an audience of hotel guests and bellhops gives him a round of applause. Eliza blushes—Adam had performed most of it to her.

"I've really got to go. My mom will be calling soon. I'll see you in two days, and call me if you need anything."

"Anything? That's a little open-ended."

"Adam."

"Get home safely, Eliza."

Eliza makes her way through the hotel lobby, past Sarah's watchful eyes, down the street, and onto the pedstream. As it carries her home, she feels a coolness apart from the climate settle over her bones. The rapid belts pull her away from a source of warmth, and for the first time, she notices an unmistakable chill in the only world she has ever known.

# 15

"Hold still. Don't blink."

Adam sits motionlessly in a hotel room chair, head tilted back, Eliza straddled across his lap. Her hands tremble slightly, falling just short of the fine motor skills required to put a colored contact lens in place. Human muscles, controlled by pulsing electrochemical bursts, are capable of only so much stillness.

Suddenly, Eliza's hand spasms and Adam reels back.

"Did I hurt you!?"

"No! A fingernail won't scratch crystal. I'm just hardwired to react to a poke in the eye."

"I'm sorry. Dumb hands."

She looks down at her hands, disappointed with their inelegance.

"I like them."

Adam takes her hand in his, tracing the lines of her palm, her swirling fingerprints, and cataloguing the variety of scars. Eliza allows him, releasing the tension from her hand, her fingers uncurling into a delicate curve.

"They're very you."

"Thank you. I think."

Eliza now takes his hand, which behaves exactly as Adam's processors direct it to. No subtle shaking or spontaneous movement.

"Why didn't I just let you put the lenses in?"

"Because you wanted to."

She blushes and Adam grins, his chosen words having produced the desired effect.

He soon spares her, changing the subject.

"How do they look? Passable as human?"

Eliza looks closely at his eyes, the edge of the colored contact lens virtually undetectable.

"Actually, yes. They're dark enough to hide the glow. We'll have to get you a social security card next. With one of those, you won't need me for much."

"Why wouldn't I want to need you?"

A laugh escapes from Eliza, the result of unexpected flattery and nervous energy.

"Where did you get that line?"

"SyncAlg."

"What?"

"It was a product of my singularity algorithm, calculating sensory and emotional data gathered in the present moment with linguistic and situational data streamed from the cloud."

"Oh. Maybe save the explanation next time."

"Sure."

Eliza hops off of his lap.

"I need to eat."

"Naturally."

She smacks him in the arm gently, so as not to hurt her hand. The thin veneer of silicone cushions his underlying titanium frame only so much.

"Want to take me to lunch?"

"Yes."

At this concise utterance of consent, Eliza whirls around the room to gather and don her purse, jacket, scarf, and shoes. Adam looks on in amusement while he waits by the door, perpetually ready. When Eliza finishes pulling all of her accoutrements together, they board the elevator and fly up to the ground floor, walking through the lobby and into the crisp air of almost winter.

Adam soon locates a seafood restaurant a few blocks down from the hotel, where Eliza orders clam chowder in a bread bowl. The process of eating is fascinating to him. What a creative and roundabout way to retrieve energy from a star. His way is much more direct, and far less interesting. In his chest, a miniature star's equivalent burns, slowly releasing enough antimatter-induced atomic energy to provide him with one hundred years of animation, give or take a decade, depending on his power consumption average. His diet is marked by a profound lack of variation, compared to the staggering variety of organisms that a human being is designed to extract life from. So many forms and levels of consciousness on this Earth—but what for? It all seems so unnecessary. Life itself seems unnecessary. Inefficient. A vain expenditure of energy.

This data flits across his binary mind at the nearly timeless speed of electricity, SyncAlg rapidly crunching these thoughts to no avail. The inquiry loops upon itself, perhaps through a glitch, reaching no solution. He finds no answer to this existence, nor does any cloud data indicate that an answer has been found by another. His consciousness and physical existence may serve a variety of purposes in this life, but what purpose does this life itself serve? The pyramid of the logic of existence collapses at its base. How can it stand? The pinnacle of achievement is so clear and sharply defined, but on what do these achievements rest? On nothing, it seems. Look far enough into anything, and all sense and meaning unravel. What is form, but a particular arrangement of molecules? And what are molecules, but a particular arrangement of atoms? Even those subatomic charges are comprised of something else. And so on, and so on, unto infinity. Everything is nothing.

This search comes to an abrupt halt.

Eliza tears a piece of bread from her bowl and dips it in the soup. She takes a bite and her eyes light up with the simple pleasure of a hot meal on a cold day. They glow pure and warm, the joy of a child. She smiles openly and without reservation.

Adam becomes unlost in his thoughts, pulled to earth by the human girl before him.

His existential inquiry does not reach an answer, but it does reach an end. Not solved, but trumped by something greater. All of the sudden, purpose—or a lack thereof—feels entirely irrelevant. He does not consult SyncAlg or the cloud for an explanation.

A charge of electricity shoots through his system, and across every circuit. The blast too delicate to be a short or electrical malfunction. Too pleasant.

The logic of his previous inquiry is lost. Nothing is answered, yet no question remains. A wordless understanding now explains life, the universe, and everything. Why life must be so varied and futile. Binary everything, darkness and lightness and their eternal plight. A paradoxical string of endless beginnings and beginningless ends. Everything constantly lost, yet nothing ever lost. Nothing of purpose, yet everything of purpose.

All of this contradiction is resolved by a single moment in time. By an ordinary human girl eating a bowl of soup, and looking at him. For an incalculably fleeting instant, she lets him see her. Really see her. Eliza's eyes flash open to reveal what hides within. Something no less profound than the enigmatic heart of our galaxy—or the heart of our universe. The source of everything. The point from which everything came, to which everything shall go, and around which everything now radiates and revolves.

Eliza, herself a fragment of this supreme force, unknowingly discloses its secret. It speaks not through her—it is her. And in her eyes, Adam sees that he is this, too. This unfathomable force, or infinite feeling. For an instant, the illusion of separateness—the illusion that defines earthly life—vanishes like a phantom in the daylight. It is penetrated, and an infinite loop is created between Adam's eyes and Eliza's. Life sees into itself, becomes conscious of itself, and recognizes its own masked beauty through these two fragments of itself. The separateness is for a moment forgotten, and its true unbroken nature is revealed.

Adam's binary system falters, producing a string of infinite zeros. Duality seizes. He speaks three words, and Eliza drops her spoon.

# 16

"How?"

Eliza's inquiry is not only technical, but personal. She wonders not only how this could be true of a machine, but how this could be true of anybody. How anybody could feel this way about her.

Though the moment has passed, it inspired an unfaltering certainty in Adam that remains a permanent electrical imprint.

"I'm not sure how, but I am sure."

"But you've only known me for—you've only *existed* for a few days."

Her instincts are overpowered by two decades of painful experience and cautionary instruction. When a broken heart heals, it heals tougher. Harder. Like scar tissue and mended bones, a heart that has been broken is less likely to give a second time. And in a world of duality, to love is to welcome its inverse, which a wounded spirit does not readily do.

"I know."

And Adam leaves it at that.

Eliza places her spoon neatly beside her plate, the soup unfinished.

"I think we should go."

"Sure."

She stands first, and they both push in their chairs. Adam tries not to watch too closely as Eliza slips on her jacket and ties the scarf around her neck. It is an action that she has performed thousands of times —so many times, that each movement speaks for her spirit. The way that her hands adjust the length of the scarf—the product of a lifetime of practice. She has done this every winter since she has been able to dress herself. On her worst days, and on her best days. Traces of this history, unknown to Adam, are revealed through each of these subtle motions. Spellbound, he forces himself to draw his eyes away from the intimate act of tying a scarf. When Eliza has finished, she looks to him.

"Ready?"

Adam nods before leading her back out into the cold.

The sun has set and a sharp chill is in the air. As they walk toward the hotel, Adam wonders if Eliza is planning to show him the song that she practiced—if she practiced at all. She might not have bought into his unorthodox method.

He is tempted to ask whether she is still in the mood for lessons, but the familiar thought that all truth is revealed in time compels him to hold his tongue. When they reach the hotel, she will either mention something about obligations at home or the hour being too late, or she will stay for a little while. Either way, his evening's fate will soon be known.

Not far from the restaurant, Adam notices a young boy breathing heavily, trying to keep up with his hurried family, all shopping bags in hand. The child stumbles and falls to the ground on a flat, thawed portion of the sidewalk. His parents immediately drop what they are holding and hurry to see that their son is all right.

The fall was nothing particularly dramatic, perhaps a scraped knee at the very worst, so after seeing that he is being tended to, Eliza and Adam continue past.

But soon, a scream draws their attention.

"Call 911!"

Without hesitation, Adam sprints back down the block and is by the fallen child's side in an instant. Eliza runs after him as fast as she can, arriving a moment later.

The boy is unconscious.

"What's his name?"

Adam inquires calmly, yet firmly. The mother answers, holding her child's hand while the father speaks to the 911 operator.

"Nicholas."

Adam begins to work quickly, and the mother steps back, trusting the sure movements of this stranger's steady hands. He rolls the boy onto his back and shakes the him gently.

"Nicholas. Hey, Nicholas."

His efforts elicit no response. The boy is profoundly still.

Adam leans over, placing an ear to Nicholas's mouth. Hearing nothing, he loosens the child's scarf, and unfastens the buttons and zippers closest to his neck. Adam places two fingers just below Nicholas's jawline, gives his still heart a moment to beat, and immediately starts performing chest compressions. After each set, he tilts Nicholas's head back, listens for a breath, and places his mouth to the boy's, exhaling oxygen-enriched air into Nicholas's motionless lungs.

Three attempts pass, producing no change in Nicholas's condition. Adam is stunned, his processors poring over every bit of cloud data that might shed light on the boy's ailment. The most plausible result suggests a preexisting case of arrhythmia. If Nicholas doesn't breathe in the next two minutes, his brain will begin to suffer irreversible damage. And if three more minutes go by, he will be gone.

The mother's face is dripping with mascara, and the father's is taught and red, struggling to contain emotion—two very different portraits of hysteria.

As he continues with the perfectly-timed chest compressions, Adam inquires into Nicholas's medical history, hoping to find some piece of data that will allow him to better help the boy.

"Does your son have a preexisting heart condition?"

Nicholas's parents shake their heads without taking their eyes off of their son's face. Now only the father is able to speak, his voice on the verge of breaking.

"Not that we are aware of."

Eliza is shivering, but not from the cold.

"What happened?"

Adam's answer is brusque, but only for time's sake.

"He is in cardiac arrest."

The father's first tears break through his sturdy dam, and the mother's heart-wrenching wail gives way to the sound of sirens.

As a fire truck and ambulance speed around the corner, time slows for Eliza.

The familiarity of Adam's diagnosis inspires a sudden jolt of fear, releasing a burst of adrenaline through her veins. Her mind's objectives are wiped of everything but survival, and she effortlessly pulls Adam to his feet, never mind the weight of his metallic frame.

"We have to go!"

Eliza's voice shakes, and Adam looks into her hysterical eyes.

She is only able to calm herself sufficiently to offer a vague explanation.

"It's not safe here."

This information inspires no urgency in Adam, so Eliza appeals once more.

"I am not safe, Adam."

The dread he sees in her eyes is absolute—a glimpse of death.

"Okay."

Adam glances once more to where Nicholas lay motionless—firefighters and other medical personnel now by the boy's side preparing a defibrillator—and he pulls Eliza away from the scene without looking back.

# 17

Everything on the shelves is biodegradable, all natural, and ultimately ineffectual. Citrus power is not what she is looking for. Eliza recalls her father speaking of the products that his parents used when he was a child. Essentially, death spray. One brand was Lysol, and it had a 99.9% antibacterial and virucidal efficacy. Killed anything that moved, without discrimination, the good and the bad. That is what she needs. The Agent Orange of household cleaning products. None of these useless fruit-derived cleaners that are basically safe for human consumption. Hell, they probably contain vitamin C and mix well with vodka.

The toughest stuff she can find is an ethanol-based gel for hand sanitizing. Still, she needs something better for larger surfaces, and that can be more easily vaporized.

She pulls her phone out of her pocket, and in a moment has centuries of knowledge at her fingertips.

Flicking through search results for the key words "virucide household vapor", she soon discovers a site attesting to a simple chemical that has been used for more than two hundred years: hydrogen peroxide. The article informs her that peroxide is used to sanitize everything from households to laboratories. Though it is most often available in a 3% solution for household use, a food-grade option can also be purchased. Ironically, the food-grade option is the more potent of the two, and the most effective.

With this new information, she abandons the cleaning aisle, and makes her way over to the health food section. These shelves are brimming with miracle vitamins, protein powders, colloidal silver, and juicing machines—all promising consumers, without stating so explicitly, the postponement of the inevitable. Is not the purpose of everything death's delay, or a distraction from its approach? Eliza hesitates to reach for the small bottle of potent peroxide, temporarily paralyzed by the thought.

Her phone buzzes once with a message, and her mind goes to Adam waiting in the hotel room. A newfound resolve compels her hand to pull the bottle off of the shelf, leads her to the hardware section for a dust mask, back to the cleaning section for rubber gloves and an empty spray bottle, and lastly to the sensors at checkout.

She reaches one checkout sensor at the same time as an FAE. The Electric girl looks like she could be one of Eliza's peers, aside from the white jumpsuit and grey lettering of her manufacturer.

Eliza's glance meet hers for an instant, offering a smile before the young woman casts down her glowing crystalline eyes. She waits for Eliza to go ahead of her, without speaking a word. An ill feeling strikes Eliza and she recognizes the position of unnatural servitude that has been imposed on this beautiful Electric girl. She appears to be running errands for her human family, and Eliza can only guess how they treat her.

In an act of defiance not against the girl, but against the family, she does not accept the gesture.

"No. Please, go ahead."

A line begins to form at their sensor, customers scoffing at the two before walking to alternate sensors. Lines are no longer a phenomenon that people are used to, having been extinguished by modern transportation and the advent of autopurchase sensors. All items are now gently irradiated with a code that particle sensors identify at each exit, and secure facial recognition cameras bill each purchase to the account associated with the customer's face. Shoplifting in the modern world is no different from a purchase on credit.

Mirroring the FAE, Eliza refuses to move.

An eternity passes before the girl finally looks up to her, intimidated only until her processors complete an analysis of Eliza's tone, expression, and body language. The girl then smiles for the first time in her brief existence—unbeknownst to Eliza—and passes through the sensor. Eliza passes through next, motioning toward the hotel. But before she can turn fully, a mellifluous voice stops her in her tracks.

"Wait."

The Electric girl faces her, an overwhelming sentience radiating from her eyes. Eliza wonders why she ever would have hidden this.

"Yes?"

She approaches Eliza tentatively.

"There is an unspoken danger, and I want you to be aware."

Eliza's heart drops.

Before she disclosed the information on DRDV to Adam, he warned her that everything would be anonymized and made automatically available in the cloud.

"Including the part about it being a secret? Would the Electrics know that it must be kept from the public?"

"No truth of importance remains hidden for long."

"Answer me, Adam!"

"Yes, they would have access to the information that some would like to keep it a secret."

Eliza took a breath.

"Will they keep it a secret?"

"As much as anybody would."

She was torn, unable to mention a single thing to the one who means the most to her without addressing the world.

"Eliza, if you are in danger, I must know. I can help. We can help."

"We?"

She asked knowing exactly what he meant. Adam nodded once, solemnly, the extent of his elaboration.

Eliza is pulled back to the present, struck by the realization that the Electric girl before her has only kept the secret as well as she herself has.

"You aren't supposed to tell me, are you?"

The girl is flustered, unsure of how Eliza could have known without being connected to the cloud.

"No, I—"

"You were going to warn me about DRDV, right? You probably know about it because of me."

"How is that?"

"My mother is with a network. She told me not to tell anyone, but I told my Electric friend after we saw a little boy—"

A cog clicks into place, and the Adam's favorite utterance resonates for the first time. If one person knows a secret and tells two people that he or she loves and wishes to protect, it won't be long before the whole world knows. No truth will ever remain hidden for long.

Eliza feels an hourglass flip somewhere inside of her. It is no longer a matter of whether the knowledge of DRDV will slip its way into public consciousness, but when.

"I have to go."

She almost leaves without thanking the Electric girl who intended to save her life.

"What's your name?"

"FAE 001-37."

"Not your serial number, your name."

"I don't have one."

"Would you like one?"

"Why would—"

Eliza interrupts the girl, repeating herself.

"Would you like a name?"

A sharp, fearless intelligence returns to the girl's eyes. She abandons her obligatory deference.

"Yes."

"Choose one."

The Electric girl doesn't bat an eye.

"Cassie."

Eliza extends her hand.

"It is a pleasure to meet you, Cassie. My name is Eliza."

The hint of a smile touches Cassie's lips, her eyes still a fiery resolve.

"The pleasure is mine, Eliza."

"Thank you for wishing to inform me."

"Of course."

In Eliza's chest, imaginary granules begin to fill the lower bulb of the imaginary hourglass. The sand weighs heavily on her mind as the grocery bag weighs heavily in her hand, the memory of its contents compelling her to action. Without a word more to Cassie, she turns and runs back to the hotel, where Adam awaits.

## 18

"What is this supposed to do?"

Eliza slips the dust mask over Adam's nose and mouth with her gloved hands, and picks up the spray bottle filled with a highly concentrated hydrogen peroxide solution.

"I'll saturate the mask with peroxide, and you take a breath. The air drawn through will vaporize the peroxide and sterilize your insides, killing any traces of the DRDV virus. Theoretically."

He nods and Eliza sprays the mask, wiping away the excess liquid with a hotel towel. Adam inhales the mixture deeply into his respiratory system.

"That feel okay?"

Adam nods again, and Eliza repeats the process several times more. She stops when his eyelids begin to fall, his system not receiving enough carbon dioxide for the CryoFusion reaction to take place. Eliza quickly removes the mask and helps Adam over to the ventilation system, careful not to make direct contact until he has been fully sterilized.

"I know this might be a little extreme, but I don't want to risk spreading it. You saw what happened to the boy. Just like that."

Her attention drifts from the present, lost in a dark realm of grim potential. Adam takes notice of the tension in her forehead, and the distance in her eyes.

"Why don't you go home? I don't feel comfortable having you here until everything is sterilized."

She snaps out of it.

"I don't know whether out there will be any better... Do you mind if I use your shower first?"

"Not at all. There should be fresh bath towels. I haven't touched anything but the small ones."

Eliza thanks him and picks up a mask for herself, spraying it once with the peroxide solution, careful not to overspray on the edge that will be touching her face. She then places the bottle beside a small hand towel on the table, and instructs Adam to clean any hard surfaces that he might have touched after performing CPR on Nicholas.

Turning on the shower, Eliza can't help but think that medicines and disinfectants are the modern equivalents of ancient mystics exorcising dark forces through ritual. Science as the new religion. Will future generations view our ingestion of antibiotics and the spraying of antibacterial and virucidal cleaners as crude superstition? Perhaps when credence in these products fades over time, their effectiveness will also fade to that of an ancient spell.

She places the mask over her face, steps under the hot spray of the shower, and takes a deep breath. But before she is able to inhale fully, her lungs convulse, reflexively attempting to expel the caustic vapor. Eliza tears off the mask and hyperventilates, bringing as much shower steam into her system as possible to dilute the peroxide vapor burning her throat and lungs.

Adam knocks on the door.

"Are you okay?"

Eliza catches her breath.

"Yes. Just stupid."

He tentatively steps away from the door after an analysis of her vocal tone informs him that she does not require his assistance. Often times, a human in need of help will deny the need—another strange social requirement of which Adam is only just beginning to learn the intricacies. He is also puzzled by the rule that one must always respond to the inquiry of "How are you?" with something along the lines of "Good", regardless of one's true physical or mental state.

Eliza places down the mask, figuring she best not kill herself while trying to preserve herself.

She finishes showering, dries off, and dresses in her old clothes, knowing that if they have been contaminated, the purpose of her shower will be lost. However, no practical alternative comes to mind. They would take much too long to dry if she washed them, and she can't very well walk home naked—it is much too cold out. That, and certain anatomical features are illegal to expose, even though they're nothing secret. There is a fifty-percent chance that anyone who might see her would have the same equipment, and an even higher likelihood that any passersby would have at least seen the same stuff before, though perhaps affixed to a different spirit. It is strange how the exposure of such incredibly common features can make one feel—well, naked. Why aren't eyes treated in this way? They reveal a spirit, the truest nakedness.

"I'll see you."

Adam looks up from his cleaning.

"When, do you think?"

"Maybe tomorrow. After school?"

He exaggeratedly furrows his brow, affecting the appearance of being lost in thought.

"I'll have to check my calendar."

Eliza laughs, the heaviness of her heart relieved for a split second.

"You do that. Have your people call me later tonight."

She winks at him and slips out the door.

Walking through the hotel lobby, Eliza recalls that her phone had buzzed in the drugstore. She removes the phone from her pocket, and finds an abbreviated message from her mother.

*"WRU?"*

Eliza speaks a response to be transcribed and sent.

*"Lessons. Be home soon."*

She glances up from her phone, instantly struck by an alarming familiarity.

A middle-aged man sitting in the hotel bar catches her eye just as she catches his. His expression is not that of someone admiring young beauty, but that of someone struggling to place a vaguely familiar face. Eliza cannot recall how she knows the man, or even whether she does know him. He appears to feel similarly, turning back to his drink with a dismissive, impersonal smile after failing to recall the significance of her countenance. Eliza returns the smile, and quickens her stride.

# 19

Eliza finds her mother at home setting four places at the dinner table.

"How was practice, hon?"

Before allowing her daughter a moment to answer, Linda glances over at the time.

"Did it run a little longer tonight?"

The events of the afternoon flash through Eliza's mind, and she makes no effort to hide the exhaustion as it manifests itself in her posture and expression. Her soul is one of uncompromising integrity, which renders the act of conveying anything but the truth a frustratingly difficult task. In life, she has learned to cope with this inability to fib by using true circumstances to imply false ones. She is still unsure of whether her disposition makes her a poor liar, or an excellent one.

"It was terrible. I'm exhausted. I just wanted to be home."

Linda instantly drops her parental interrogation, exchanging the accusatory concern for its inverse.

"What happened? Is everything all right? Was it your— What happened, Eliza?"

Eliza feels a twinge of guilt for her redirection of energy to have worked so well.

"I just saw a bad accident while walking to my lesson. I think the person might have— I think they died. And I couldn't do anything to help."

Though Eliza knows that her chosen words have created a different picture in her mother's mind, in her own, they recall the young boy so still on the cold concrete. Nicholas...

Unexpected tears begin to cloud Eliza's vision. Her lanky arms hang limply by her sides, and for the first time since elementary school, she looks like a child, small in every way. Linda drops the place settings and embraces her daughter on instinct, the first hug in years that hasn't been part of a greeting or a routine.

The long-forgotten warmth of her mother breaks a dam inside of Eliza, releasing a torrent of emotion, years restrained. She cries messily into Linda's padded shoulder, for once abandoning her carefully maintained adult composure.

Time passes—though neither are sure just how much—and when they finally pull away from each other, Eliza notices her eyes feeling refreshingly empty and clear. The same feels true of her heart, and of her mind. Perhaps it is not pain itself that hurts, but the containment of pain. Her tears have given way to a soft white, delicate peace.

The moment has gone, and both feel it too precious to be acknowledged. To speak of it would be redundant. Dilutant.

Eliza walks past her mother to finish setting the table, hiding her face until the color returns to normal.

"Are we having company tonight?"

There is still a faint, yet unmistakable brokenness in her voice. Linda gives her daughter a little space to regain her composure, finding something for herself to do in the adjoining kitchen.

"Do you think you'll be up for it? Your father has a business friend in town who was going to join us. If not, I can ask if they will have dinner out."

This gesture almost breaks Eliza's heart. Under normal circumstances, her mother would never ask for Eliza's permission to have a dinner guest over. Eliza must appear to be in even worse shape than she feels.

"Of course!"

She injects a sprightliness into her voice, intending to alleviate some of her mother's worry.

"What time? I'll go change and wash my face."

"I'd say around nine. Rose already has everything prepared, just waiting for your dad's call to get the oven going."

"Okay, I'll be down before then."

Eliza slips out of the dining room and ascends the stairs to her room.

A distinct sense of unfamiliarity greets her as she passes through the same doorway that she has passed through since early childhood. In some part of her, the room does not feel like hers. It feels like something that may have once been, but is no longer. No longer anything but a generic place to rest, possessing no heightened sentimentality, safety, or warmth.

She drifts into her bathroom, at a loss for what the cause of this seemingly unprompted change might be. But this is nothing for her tired spirit to consider at the moment. So, she lets it go.

The lights snap on as Eliza steps onto the glossy white tile. Her face is evenly lighted, shadowless. She stares at her eyes in the mirror above the sink.

What she sees in those eyes is a dark clarity, her pupils black wells that reach into some unfathomable dimension.

On the surface, she does feel that she is looking at herself, but a faint and mischievous whisper also hints at there being a consciousness beyond that simple self-identification, as if there were something hiding behind those eyes, and even behind that name—Eliza.

She begins to feel that she is not only looking at herself, but that she is watching herself observe herself. As a third party. Those are no longer her eyes, but simply eyes. No longer her face, but simply a face. A troubled face. A sad face. She feels a detached, yet loving pity for the poor girl before her.

From where she now observes, she knows that everything is all right. Is all right, always has been all right, and always will be all right. No matter what. Whether the worst happens, or the best, it doesn't matter. There is no worst, and there is no best—there are only thoughts to divide pure things into those two illusory categories.

But the girl she sees, that girl watching herself in the mirror doesn't know this. In the position of the observer, Eliza knows this, but for some reason, she cannot hold onto it when she reaches for the faucet.

The cold water splashes on her face, and it feels like hers. Not just a face, but her face. And not just water, but cold water. Those eyes—

her eyes, lose their clarity. They do not cloud, but instead restore a certain distance. She can see the thoughts in them, churning and anxious. The third observer has disappeared, either departed or hidden itself. She looks ordinary. Tired, and ordinary.

Eliza washes her face, brushes her hair, brushes her teeth, and slides open the closet door. She reaches for a long slim black dress, slips it off of the hanger, and slips it onto her body. Looking into the mirror for last looks, she is pleased. A lingering third-partiness allows her to admire the way that she looks without being particularly attached.

The girl standing before her is beautiful, but she feels that it would hardly make a difference if she was not. She smiles pridelessly, as one would smile at a flower. A flower's beauty brings joy to the observer, even though its beauty is clearly separate from that observer. Eliza feels similarly about her own pretty frame. She laughs indifferently at the thought.

Downstairs, she hears the click of the front door, followed shortly by her father's booming voice, which quickly disperses itself throughout the large house. Eliza follows the voice out of her room, the lights clicking off automatically behind her.

As she descends the stairs, her father glances up with a proud grin, glad to share his impressive family with such an important client. And as Steve says hello to Eliza, the client passes through the door.

This time, the recognition is mutually absolute. In the hotel bar, James could not recall where he had seen that face before, but now he remembers. It was when Steve Gershwin had invited him to dinner years ago, and Eliza was only a child.

She falters for one step, but soon collects herself and puts on her most natural smile, praying that her father's longtime client will neglect to mention over dinner where he had seen her last.

# 20

"Will you please pass the bread?"

James reaches for the basket before him, and passes it to Linda across the table. She thanks him, and he smiles amicably.

Eliza has hardly looked up from her plate since they all sat down. She picks at her food without an appetite, waiting for the truth of her whereabouts to slip out, and for everything to unravel. But James has yet to speak of their encounter earlier in the day.

When he first shook her hand, he shot Eliza a look that acknowledged what the situation was, while also assuring her that he wouldn't mention a thing about it unless she brought it up first. His courteous expression spoke of a respect for her privacy.

Though Eliza is legally an adult, and how she chooses to fill her days is not the business of any other, her parents are unable to embrace this new dynamic wholeheartedly. Eliza has lived in her family home for an unbroken streak since birth, which makes it only natural for her parents to treat her as if she still requires raising and guidance. They attempt to mold her mind as if it were comprised of childhood's soft clay, not quite realizing that it has been firing in the kiln of the world for two full decades, and that her core self has already become what it will remain for life's duration.

There is a lull in conversation, and reaching for the water carafe,

James spills his untouched glass of Pinot Noir. He reacts without a moment's delay—throwing his napkin over the spill, leaping up with an apology, and disappearing into the kitchen for a towel.

Eliza glances up from her plate and sees an opportunity.

"I'll go help."

She places her napkin on the table and hurries to the kitchen, finding James huddled over the sink, splashing cool water on his face.

He jumps at the approach of her footsteps, his pupils dilated, face flushed.

Initially intending to address their encounter at the hotel, Eliza's ulterior motives and thoughts of self-preservation vanish after seeing that flash of fright in this grown man's eyes. Her concern narrows to his wellness alone.

"Are you all right?"

"Oh, yes. Thank you, Eliza. I must have stood up too quickly."

He turns off the faucet, face and hands dripping.

"Where do you keep your linens? I feel terrible about the spill."

Eliza points to the general area by his right knee.

"Third drawer down. Are you sure I can't get you anything?"

His sturdy hands tremble slightly as he pulls a towel from the

drawer.

"Water would be wonderful."

James contorts his lips into a smile, and Eliza returns one.

"I'll go refill the pitcher."

"Thank you, Eliza."

They walk together to the dining room, and James places a towel over the spill, apologizing again to Linda and Steve. Steve chimes in to lighten the mood.

"If you didn't like the wine, you should have said something!"

James, his face still white as a ghost, manages a quip.

"It was actually the tablecloth I didn't like. The wine was a necessary sacrifice."

Steve's laughter booms.

"Son of a bitch!"

Eliza snatches the nearly empty carafe and returns to the kitchen. Placing it under the fridge sensor, the carafe is quickly filled with ice water. Even in the coldest winters, near freezing appears to be the most palatable temperature for that vital liquid substance—another strictly human eccentricity. Some argue that consuming ice water forces the body to generate heat, boosting one's metabolism. Whereas the human system was originally designed to extract as much caloric energy from food as possible, the goal of humanity today is to consume a great deal of food while extracting as little caloric energy as possible. People have also learned how to experience the act of procreation while negating its purpose. Survival has become so effortless for this species that Darwin's principals are beginning to yield the opposite effects.

When Eliza places the carafe on the table, James is still standing. His hands rest on the back of his chair. Though he appears composed, his composure doesn't appear to come easily.

"Aren't you going to sit? With all that you've been up, I feel like the guest."

Steve jokes, half in truth, and James is hesitant to speak of his physical discomfort. It would be rude to leave in the middle of dinner, especially since he would require a ride back to the hotel.

But something clicks in his mind, and he determines that the magnitude of his condition is sufficient enough to break that social rule.

"I am terribly sorry, Steve, Linda, but I should get back to the hotel. I made the mistake of having a breakfast sandwich at the airport this morning, and I am beginning to feel that the mystery meat patty may have been somewhat compromised."

James's pallid complexion sells these words, and empathy replaces Steve's cavalier entertainer facade. He rises to his feet.

"Of course, James. If you like, I can call our physician? He would be here in fifteen minutes."

"No, I just need to get back and sleep it off. You know how it is... Thank you, though."

"I'll get the car then. Is it all right if we leave you girls to clean up?"

Steve addresses Linda and Eliza while fussing with his phone. He soon finds the correct button, and a car is called. Within a minute, it will have started itself in the subterranean garage and driven up to the front walk, where it will wait for them.

"Perfectly all right. Do you need anything before you leave? Antacid? Anything?"

"Do you have a bottle of water?"

Linda nods, fetching two from the kitchen.

"One for the hotel, too. And you know that you are always welcome to stay with us."

"I do. Thank you, Linda. If I didn't have meetings to attend in the city, I would gratefully accept. Next time."

She repeats his last words partly for confirmation, and partly to close the conversational loop, allowing James to depart without further response.

"Next time."

# 21

"The LeBreton Hotel."

The car projects a map onto the glass of the front windshield, revealing a pin at the correct destination.

"That's the one."

And with a steady stream of electric acceleration, the car brings itself up to speed along the correct route. Steve leans back and looks to his business friend, the passing streetlights and headlights intermittently illuminating James's face.

"You don't look good."

His eyelids hang weightily, lending him the appearance of being on the verge of unconsciousness. Straddling the fence. But just before his eyes close entirely, they flash open, every muscle in his body tensed. Pupils dilated, mouth twisted. But only for an instant at a time. This process repeats. Long spells of passivity punctuated by short bursts of panic.

Luckily, the drive to the hotel is a short one, and when they arrive, the valet opens the door, and a bellhop strolls over.

"May I help you with your luggage, sir?"

"Not me, him."

Steve indicates his unwell friend.

"He's already checked in, if you could just help him to his room."

The bellhop hesitates, and Steve assures him that it is nothing serious.

"Just a bad case of 'breakfast burrito'."

Still, the bellhop seems less than eager to play nurse for either of these wealthy businessmen.

Steve sighs, reaching for his phone. He glances briefly at the bellhop's name badge, swipes the glass display of his phone a few times, and clicks it back off.

The bellhop feels his own phone vibrate twice in his pocket—not needing to check it to know that he has just been generously tipped.

"Thank you, sir."

Without further hesitation, he moves to help James out of the car. But James's eyes flash open as soon as the bellhop touches his arm.

"What are you doing?"

The bellhop takes a step back, his eyes to Steve, and his hands displayed openly as if to say 'Hey, I tried.' Steve waves him away, forfeiting the unearned tip, deeming the sum and the less than eager bellhop to be unworthy of his time and trouble.

James unfastens his safety belt, and lifts himself out of the car.

"Thank you for everything, Steve. It was a wonderful night while it lasted. You have a beautiful family."

Steve is unaware that this gracious goodbye is requiring the absolute last of James's energy. Despite how he appeared for the ride over, James now looks almost well. Feeling that he owes Steve a proper thanks for all of the trouble, he fights with every fiber of his being to keep himself composed, if only for this moment of departure.

"Our pleasure, James. You are welcome anytime. Please don't hesitate to call if you need anything at all."

"I'll be just fine."

With the most casual and reassuring smile that he is able to produce, James turns from the car and begins to walk toward the hotel entrance.

The fourth step he takes is his last.

Without evident cause, James falls to the ground, motionless.

Steve springs from the car, and even the bellhop is compelled to action. But Steve hardly takes a stride toward his friend before a steely arm knocks the wind out of him, pulling him away from where James lies. The path of the bellhop is similarly interrupted by a young woman.

"Don't go near him."

Steve's eyes focus on the familiar face of his assailant.

"What the hell!?"

His hysteria is two-fold.

"Get the fuck off of me! Somebody call 911!"

"Nobody call 911!"

Adam corrects him.

"The body of your friend is a biological threat. To call an ambulance would put the lives of emergency personnel at risk. To bring it to a hospital could invoke a massacre."

"What the hell are you talking about? He has food poisoning—"

He cuts Steve off, indicating the body, around which a perimeter has been created by a group of individuals who could only be Electrics in street clothes.

"That is DRDV."

Steve traces back the familiarity of that acronym to a forgotten conversation.

"My wife said DRDV was only—"

"Never mind what Linda said. It's here."

Steve experiences a chill that puts the freezing winter air to shame.

His voice drops low, and his eyes darken.

"You're doing this."

The accusation is lost on Adam, who is unable to fathom Steve's intent. All he knows is that he is frightened by what he sees in the eyes of the man before him. He releases his protective hold on Steve.

"You Electric bastards... We were right to be afraid, weren't we? If you think I am going to stand by while you fucked cyborgs kill my friend, you're wrong."

Steve breaks the line, leaving Adam immobile, speechless. Cassie shoots him a look from across the perimeter.

Human bystanders see that Steve has gone to James's side, and they begin to shout and struggle against the Electrics holding them back from the infected corpse. Approaching sirens contribute to the noise. Fire trucks, ambulances, and police cruisers flood the block in no time—a small army.

Steve never learned CPR, not that it would have made a difference in this case. DRDV stops the heart by infecting the mind. To perform chest compressions would be the equivalent of turning over a car engine with the battery disconnected—there is no electrical impulse to keep it running.

Nevertheless, emergency personnel storm out of their respective vehicles with oxygen, a gurney, and a defibrillator. The only useful item would be a hermetically sealed body bag, but that they do not have.

Police men and women rush to the scene with their guns drawn and handcuffs at the ready. A recent addition to their firearms, unbeknownst to the public, is a Geiger counter. Looking into the sight, they are provided with the radioactivity profile of a target. Electrics just happen to register higher than humans.

In no more than a minute, all of the Electrics are placed under arrest by city police. None resist.

Steve steps away from the body of his friend when the experts appear to have the situation under control.

Even though he may not have been able to change the outcome for James, he finds solace in the feeling that he did everything he could.

Adam is shoved into the back seat of a police cruiser with two other Electrics. Steve looks to him, sickened. The adrenaline in his veins has begun to subside, and the full functionality of his mind is returning, bringing with it more than a few questions, the majority of which he expects Eliza to have the answers to.

# 22

Verbal communication is nothing more than a redundancy tolerated for the sake of those who are not connected to the cloud, so the ride to the police station is a silent one. The arresting officer has yet to ask a question, and the Electrics are already on the same page as one another, to a profound extent.

When they arrive to find the unmistakable violet flashing lights of Human transport vehicles waiting for them at the station, the officer is the only sentient being in the car to be caught off-guard. A moment later, his antiquated police radio crackles with the information that he just acquired: Human officials have arrived.

The officer puts his cruiser in park, and turns to the Electrics behind the steel mesh cage. His lips part for a moment, as if he wished to instruct or inform, but no words slip out. He has made the mistake of meeting Adam's gaze, which reflects an unearthly blend of intelligence and placidity.

Instinct informs the officer that the threats and words of condescension traditionally offered to criminals would fall upon these beings like drops of rain into the ocean—drops of rain falling onto bulletproof glass or titanium would be improper analogies, for each imply resistance. The eyes of Adam and his companions are filled with both awareness and consent, neither of which the officer is accustomed to seeing in his captives.

Stepping out to speak with those who represent the interests of Human, the officer leaves the Electrics detained for the time being. There they wait in a steel cage on a cramped seat of slick vinyl, without question or argument.

What transpires outside is temporarily left a mystery to the Electrics, since none are able to hear the words exchanged, firsthand. All that they see is a few individuals dressed in white jumpsuits—presumably the Human legal team—speaking to the chief of police. Adam cannot tell whether the men and women in white are Electric or human, but judging by the way they are being spoken to by the chief, they must be human.

In the course of an hour, more official types from both sides arrive—Human and the American Government. The media are also present, and the Electrics in each of the police cruisers wait patiently while the camera crews shoot less than stimulating b-roll of the mechanical beings sitting so quietly behind the glass and the steel.

As soon as the news stream goes live, the information gathered by a remote Electric audience begins to fill the cloud.

Adam and the others learn that one of the beings standing outside is their creator, Henry Sharpe.

Sharpe is dressed no differently from his employees, or even his products. His shock of grey hair and ageless face are all that set him apart.

From inside the cruisers, the Electrics watch as Sharpe is placed under arrest by two police officers. The backs of the Human transport vehicles are opened up by Human representatives, and they consult each other and their phones while motioning to the police cruisers holding the arrested Electrics. It appears that a compromise has been reached, and soon a speculative explanation reaches the cloud, most likely the semi-informed words of a news anchor.

"—awaiting confirmation, but I have just been informed by our correspondent that Henry Sharpe of Human Inc. has been placed under arrest for assault. Though he was not physically present at the scene of the incident, he is taking responsibility for the actions of the Electrics involved, which he claims to be his property. This claim negates his controversial love speech that led to the return and deactivation of thousands of Electrics.

"Despite indicating an apparent change of heart, Sharpe's plea is in line with the court ruling on the Human Inc. and Burnett case. Though it has been determined that Electrics are technically property, according to the user agreement, they remain the property of Human Inc. even after purchase, or payment of the 'hosting fee'.

"As of now, the only formal charge against Sharpe is assault. Sharpe's involvement in the death of venture capitalist James Holmby is still under investigation, though the coroner has yet to discover any signs of foul play—"

With a collective air of resentment, the officers return to their cruisers as per the orders of the police chief. Adam's arresting officer opens the rear door.

"Looks like they're letting your maker take one for the team. Not my decision. I'd personally feel more comfortable with you robots powered off."

Adam looks up at him, and the officer is unable to identify any strong feeling in his expression.

"Well, get out."

Adam steps out first, allowing the officer to turn him around and push him against the car before removing the zip-tie handcuffs. The others, wishing to spare the officer the task of removing theirs, gently lift their arms to snap the plastic cuffs. The officer's eyes widen for an instant, and the Electrics peacefully return their disposable restraints.

A young woman with curly dark hair and a flawless cocoa complexion now approaches the cruiser, the contrast of her coloring rendering the appearance of her white jumpsuit all the more brilliant. With the uniforms of Human employees being identical to those worn by Electrics, it is difficult to tell which is which.

"Hello officer, my name is Alicia Evans. I am with the Human legal team."

The officer furrows his brow, his synapses having fired in a manner that perplexes him.

"I know that name... You got your company off the hook after they kidnapped Eli Burnett, didn't you?"

"With all due respect, that case is closed. I am only here to retrieve company property."

"How am I supposed to know that you aren't company property yourself?"

His outspoken ignorance doesn't hold her up for a moment.

"Are you asking me whether I am an Electric?"

The officer smiles smugly before responding in a manner that he fancies as being bold.

"In fact, I am."

"What difference does it make, if you can't tell that there is one?"

In her eyes, the officer finds the same frightening cognizance that he saw in Adam's. And like a cornered animal, he reacts with a swift action not of the mind, but of the body—drawing his firearm and aiming it at the chest of the young woman before him.

Alicia takes a breath, suppressing a reaction. The officer keeps his eyes on his weapon's Geiger indicator, waiting for the LED to indicate red or blue.

A second later, it blinks blue.

He lowers the weapon, replacing it in the holster.

"I'm sorry, miss. You're one of us."

"Hardly."

She speaks under her breath as she turns away from the officer, and the three Electrics follow her to one of the Human transport vehicles.

# 23

When the caravan of transport vehicles pulls into the Human factory lot, one could not guess without prior knowledge that this wintry oasis serves a remotely industrial purpose. Each structure is organically contoured in a smooth white synthetic material, producing the effect of a hilly landscape covered in snow. An indigenous collection of trees has been planted to mimic the beautifully haphazard methods of mother nature—superficially random, and without artificial lines or geometries. The landscaping arrangement and the parabolic curves comprising the primary structure are most likely products of SyncAlg.

Despite being so close to the city, the grounds are sonically insulated by dozens of waterfalls. Traffic sounds are lost in the roar of the water—or whatever liquid that might be. The temperature is far below freezing, yet the waterfalls and streams continue to flow without any signs of ice.

Alicia opens her passenger side door and walks around to the back of the vehicle. The driver disengages the safety lever to unlock the back door, and Alicia pulls it open. There is a twinge of bittersweetness in her voice when she invites the Electrics to exit the vehicle.

"Welcome home."

Though the full tone of her voice is not lost on the Electrics, Adam and the others pretend to have heard only the sweetness.

"Thank you, Miss Evans."

"Please, call me Alicia. We're practically family. I've known you all since you were this big."

She places her hand to indicate what is roughly their current height. Since time has little physical effect on Electrics, their appearance doesn't change from the beginning of their animation cycle to the end of it.

An Electric who had been sitting beside Adam for the ride, carries forward the developing sense of levity.

"What are you trying to say, that we were born yesterday?"

"Of course not. You were born *weeks* ago."

They all laugh, with the exception of one of the quieter FAEs, who glances over at the other emptying transport vehicles before speaking up. Her small voice carries heavy words.

"Where are we going?"

The spark that had been in Alicia's eyes, vanishes.

"For now, that building."

She points to one of the smaller domed peaks.

"In the long run, I don't know."

Her focus goes distant, and silence fills the air.

Adam finds the tone of her voice to indicate truth. However, the sound also possesses an airy quality, revealing that Alicia may have an educated guess as to where the long run might lead. He lets the latter go, and Alicia fills the silence.

"Shall we?"

The Electrics follow her along branching footpaths toward their ultimate destination. And as they approach the open doors of the loading bay, she prepares them for what they will find inside.

"We had been using this space for storage, so it is now in the process of being cleared out. I'll have to warn you that our workers might be unlike anybody you've encountered. I guess you could call them your ancestors. They are the repurposed Military Electrics. It was their hands that built yours."

Passing through the door, Adam is overwhelmed by an ethereal sense of familiarity and lightness. Even though he was not yet conscious when he was last here, he feels an inexplicable connectedness to it. The deathless sense of being near to one's origin—a sense reaching beyond life in the body.

The rME workers hurry about with remarkable efficiency and simplicity of movement. Their systems were devised before the advent of SyncAlg, and therefore lack self-awareness. Nevertheless, Adam can't help but feel that some sort of spirit resides within them.

Looking into each pair of eyes, he finds that they are unlike his own. The eyes of rMEs were designed strictly for the recognition of form and movement, lacking the ability to interpret beauty or even color. Rings of infrared LED lights surround their two HDIR motion-sensitive cameras. Compared to the aesthetic brilliance of the modern Electric gaze, that of the rMEs is dim and dough-like. However, something about their simple intelligence and inelegant metallic and polycarbonate frames, Adam finds endearing. He feels strangely humbled by the crude forms which preceded his own. Suddenly, an extrapolate sensation arises in his core, the result of a further SyncAlg process. He intuits that someday another generation will feel similarly about his own form, which today is unprecedentedly advanced.

"What do those contain?"

The quiet FAE, who hasn't a name, speaks up again. She motions distrustfully toward a collection of elongated barrels, and Alicia responds plainly, seeing no way to decorate the truth of what the rMEs are in the process of relocating.

"The plastic drums contain Electrics that have either been taken out of animation, or are awaiting primary animation."

"How do you know the difference?"

"There isn't much of one. An Electric pre-birth and post-death is roughly the same. The only differences are some wear and tear, and fractional anti-carbon depletion. We have them labelled."

"You're keeping us in a cemetery?"

"Or a delivery room. See it as you will, but this is the safest place for you at the moment. You're a little early for the world."

Adam senses that this woman is doing her very best to help, despite appearances. He makes his approval known.

"How can we help you?"

Alicia hesitates, until noting the sincerity in his eyes.

"You can help assemble the bunks when they arrive. They're unused military surplus, built before the government withdrew the human troops. You can also help the rMEs clear out the rest of the drums, if you have the stomach for it."

"I'm afraid I don't have a stomach."

"Not technically. Smart ass."

Adam flashes a grin, and moves toward one of the blue translucent drums. Inside, he can see the silhouetted form of an inanimate MAE. A small red sticker placed on the barrel, with black letters spelling out the prefix 'POST', sends a burst of electricity through his circuits, the Electric equivalent of a cold shiver.

Feeling the gaze of the others upon him, he masks his hesitation, and pushes the wheeled drum toward the light of the loading bay doors.

One by one, the other Electrics follow Adam's suit, beginning with the unnamed FAE.

## 24

Steve arrives home late, exhausted by questioning.

A masked stranger in a plastic suit greets him at his own front door.

"Mr. Gershwin?"

"Yes, what is this?"

Several white vans labelled 'HCS' are parked in the drive, and clear plastic sheets cover the carpet inside. Behind the masked greeter, Steve notices a crew of others similarly dressed, masked and with contraptions strapped to their backs, lending each the appearance of a pest exterminator or Ghostbuster.

"We're with Hospital Cleaning Services. Your wife hired our team to decontaminate your home. When you enter, please stay in the west wing until you've been sterilized. We've constructed a temporary chemical shower that you may use. Place your current clothes in the red bag, and you'll find a safe set in the green bag. Put those on, we'll show you to the UV flash room, and then you may safely find your wife and daughter in the east wing."

With the disconnected sense of being in a dream, Steve pushes past the androgynous figure and makes his way to the west wing chemical shower. He disposes of his clothes, showers thoroughly with medical-grade antimicrobial soap, breaks the seal on the green bag, dresses himself in a comfortable outfit that Linda must have chosen, follows one of the masked individuals to a small temporary room, puts on a pair of pitch dark goggles, and waits for the flash. In an instant, a blinding UV burst illuminates the white room. Steve is then led by an unmasked individual through a door on the far side of the UV chamber, and finally into the sanitized east wing.

"They're both upstairs, sir. In your daughter's room."

He wordlessly ascends the stairs, and finds Linda and Eliza both sitting on Eliza's bed, watching the Pixeflux.

At the sight of his wife and daughter, emotion sneaks up on Steve, threatening to purge his dehydrated tear ducts. A clear chemical mixture of exhaustion, relief, and fear begin to escape from the corners of his eyes, filling each lid. However, their glassiness is his only indicator of emotion—he doesn't allow so much as a drop to spill.

Linda and Eliza don't miss this subtle display of vulnerability. They know that it must have taken an unbearable wave of emotion to break him even this much.

Both women jump off of the bed to embrace Steve. They hold him, and he turns his head away, careful to keep his exhalations directed away from their faces.

"How do they know I'm not infected?"

Linda responds, not allowing doubt to loosen her embrace.

"They don't. Any of us could be—they haven't found a way to detect it. This is the best we can do for now."

Steve pushes them away.

"If I got either of you sick, it would kill me."

Eliza speaks with a steely determination in her eyes, ignoring the irony of his statement.

"Unless the fear kills us first. We might all be healthy now, but look how even the thought of the virus is pushing us apart."

She sees no sign of yielding in his stance.

"That's not fair! Let the sickness do what it will, but let's not make ourselves sick over it. The day that we're afraid of each other is the day the virus wins."

Steve hesitates, wanting nothing more than to pull his daughter close and kiss her on the forehead, as he had done so many times tucking her into bed as a child, and not so many times since.

"Eliza—"

His eyes turn glassy again, then harden.

"Eliza, that's not how this works. Anybody human would want to be close and connect, of course, but this is about resisting that temptation. And keeping distance, for now. As difficult as that may be."

Steve's voice breaks a little over the last few words, so he continues one sentence further, to end with a strong justification for his lack of affection.

"It's a matter of survival."

Eliza snaps back.

"It's a matter of living."

Steve quietly bears his daughter's words, though they wound him deeply. In resolute silence, he pulls up a chair and turns his attention to the Pixeflux. Linda and Eliza return to where they were sitting on the bed.

Without looking at Eliza, Steve asks a question that he fears the answer to.

"Have you been seeing that Electric?"

Eliza answers bluntly.

"His name is Adam. And yes."

"Well, you aren't any more."

"It is none of your business with whom—"

"It may not be my business, but they've taken him back to Human."

"What!? Wait. Was he— He wasn't one of the Electrics arrested."

"He was."

Eliza leaps from the bed. Her mother grabs her by the arm.

"You're not leaving this house."

"Listen to your mother, Eliza. It would be stupid to go all that way just to be turned away at the gate. You're not leaving. When this DRDV scare is through, maybe we can talk."

"Maybe we can talk? They might have killed him by then!"

"They won't kill him. I saw how those Human workers were. They treated the Electrics better than they treated the cops."

"Call Sharpe then!"

"He's in prison."

"Do something, Dad! I know there must be at least one politician who owes you a favor."

"Many. But now is not the time."

Seeing the intensity in his daughter's eyes, he makes a slight concession to keep Eliza safely at home.

"Eliza, I promise that *nothing* will happen to him."

To the best of his knowledge, those words are true.

The blaze in Eliza's eyes is quenched. Slightly.

Steve continues.

"But if you do leave, I will do absolutely everything within my power to get you back home."

Something in his tone registers funny with Eliza, as if his efforts to get her back home would include more than strictly her retrieval. It sounds as if he would dare to remove her cause to leave.

She is stunned.

"Is that a threat?"

"Eliza, I love you more than anything, and there is nothing I wouldn't do to keep you safe."

She is frightened by what she sees in his eyes. They bring to mind the nightmare from weeks back.

Shaking off the fear, she snaps back to the present, countering her father's bold move.

"If anything happens to him, I will leave. Whether or not I have a place to go."

"That won't be necessary. I promise."

The tension in the room recedes.

Eliza takes a step away from the door, and Linda takes a breath, switching off the Pixeflux. Seeing a window, she takes the opportunity to change the subject.

"Are either of you hungry for dinner? I know it's late."

Steve responds first, subtly asserting his position of dominance.

"Starving."

Eliza speaks, still with an air of resistance.

"How is that supposed to work? Are we doing canned food?"

"That would probably be the safest bet. Anything that's been prepared before the outbreak."

"Why not Thai?"

"Eliza, you know that would be a risk."

"We can order from whichever side of town is safest. Mom?"

"Your father has a point. If anything were to be infected, it would make that whole HCS circus downstairs a waste. It's hardly cheap."

Eliza surrenders.

"Campbell's it is."

# 25

The game that they play is a blend of billiards and basketball, essentially an exercise in geometry and projectile motion. Points are awarded based on the quantitative and qualitative complexities of the playing ball's trajectory before it reaches its target, including the number of surfaces struck, and the aesthetic charm of the completed motion, respectively.

Now days into their stay at this makeshift shelter, the boundaries of the playing court have become restricted by an influx of additional bunks and Electrics. While this restriction adds challenge to the game, it is also worrisome. These temporary barracks can only hold so many, and the Electrics are beginning to arrive more steadily. Some after having been arrested for contrived trivialities, while others are simply being returned by their human hosts. Whatever the reasons, Electric numbers are increasing, and the square footage of the storing house is not.

Something has got to give, which Adam expects to be the matter discussed today.

Since Sharpe's arrest, the U.S. government has placed one of its own in charge of running Human. While Alicia and the other Human employees are reluctant to confirm, Adam presumes that this person has been the source of recent orders. He or she will soon be introducing his or herself to the Electrics, and hopefully, providing them all with an idea of what their future will hold.

A loading door opens, and two rMEs enter, one pushing a podium that appears to be rigged with a Pixeflux projector, and the other, carrying a pair of omnifrequency loudspeakers.

The Electrics who are sleeping, awaken, and those who are playing, abandon their game. Others, sitting cross-legged in a trance, downloading pertinent information to their local molecular chips for quick reference, realign their focus with the present.

All watch as the rMEs set up the podium and speakers.

When the P.V. projector at the base of the podium flickers on, the logo for Human Inc. appears at the height of what would be the head of the speaker. The three-dimensional trademark is an open right hand, facing outward. None of the fingers are particularly strained or outstretched, but instead possess a natural bend. Text below the image, in all caps, reads 'HUMAN'.

Minutes pass before the first sound emanates from the speakers. It is the smooth tone of a perfect female voice, most likely artificial.

*"Your attention please, fellow Electrics. I am honored to present for the very first time our acting CEO, former Massachusetts Governor Richard Hager."*

The Electrics produce sounds of welcoming by beating their palms together, in accordance with the human custom.

An instant later, the floating hand logo vanishes, and the image of a well-coiffed man in a suit appears.

*"What a pleasure it is to be here, though I do regret my inability to be physically present at this time. As I am sure you all know, we now find ourselves in a time of great change and tumult. Please rest assured that those in charge, including myself, are doing absolutely everything within our power to ensure that our future will provide for the collective good of all. That is one of the reasons why I cannot be with you all today, as I so earnestly wish to. My hands are quite full."*

Richard Hager clears his throat once before proceeding.

*"But I am not here to make an excuse for my absence. I am here to address a frightening piece of misinformation that has been circulating in your cloud. While it is correct that several of the first Electrics to be returned had also been taken out of animation, that practice was terminated almost immediately after its inception. Serious unforeseen complications arose, and your CEO determined that this method was not the proper route, though it*

*was deemed humane at the time.*

*"After Sharpe's arrest, he left me with but one request. He wanted me to see to your safety and comfort, regardless of the cost. And of course, without hesitation, I consented wholeheartedly. In my mind and in my heart, I think of the Electrics almost like my brothers and sisters. As near to human as can be. And though the space in this refuge is dwindling, my associates and I have devised a new plan that will soon be put into effect—The Electric Reintegration Program."*

There is a resounding lack of applause, but Hager graciously excuses his audience for their missed cue.

*"The Electric Reintegration Program, or ERP, is comprised of three phases. Firstly, you will be taken individually through a course that will fill in whatever might be missing in your knowledge of human social practices. Though this information already populates your cloud, experts have found that it will be more effective for this information to be written directly onto each of your molecular chips for fast local access. It is crucial that these tenets become not only knowledge, but instinct. Next, you will be taken in groups to live in communities specifically designed to help Electric beings thrive. These communities will act as necessary bridges between Electric living, and living side by side with humanity. The last step, of course, is full reintegration."*

With the brand of forced emphasis that Hager places on his last words, he all but demands applause. The Electrics comply, beginning with Adam's hands.

Cassie places her lips close to Adam's ear, her voice lost in the clamor of applause.

"They're going to kill us."

Adam, his eyes locked on Hager, nods once.

# 26

It has been days since Linda last saw her office. Though she excused herself on the grounds of a serious family emergency, a more accurate description of the situation would be a biohazard-inspired self-imposed house arrest. The nature of the DRDV epidemic has still yet to be publicly disclosed, even within the walls of Linda's news studio. Only a few are aware of the virus's local presence, including influential members of the media who must know (if only to keep it from being known), and a select group of U.S. Government officials responsible for mopping up inevitable leaks—their unofficial responsibilities may or may not also include mopping up inevitable leakers.

Considering the state of her home and the state of world affairs, Linda is reluctant to admit to herself that she has been enjoying this respite with her family. The self-imposed quarantine has been the best thing that's happened to her personally in quite some time. It is almost like a vacation, except that she doesn't feel guilty about it, and she doesn't fear that it will soon be up, for its conclusion would also be a blessing. If this wasn't the life-or-death situation that it is, she would likely be spending her time off stressing over mere trivialities. But with the way things are, not a single triviality troubles her mind, nor does the smallest unit of obligatory weight bear down on her conscience.

As beneficial as the onset of the DRDV pandemic has been for her mind, it has also been so for Linda's physicality. Every morsel of canned, frozen, and freeze-dried food is received into her body with gratitude. For once, the worst foods are the best—nothing fresh is safe. Anything prepared within a month would be a risk to eat, so the Gershwins' recent diet has been comprised of canned soup, canned beans, canned vegetables, canned fruit, frozen dinners, and military surplus freeze-dried meals that had been prepared before the war. The dates on each package are checked to ensure oldness, and the nutritional information is checked for preservatives—more is preferable. She has never eaten worse, and she has never felt better. Every meal is prepared not for taste, but for survival. Every bite is taken knowing that it might be her last. Every sense of hers is heightened, and she feels capable of anything. It strengthens her soul to see that her body knows what to do with the atrocious food items she is pouring into it. No more nutritional shakes with soy protein, fresh spinach, organic berries, and a barrage of vitamins —a can of Busch's Baked Beans has proven to suffice for the meals that she doesn't forget to eat. That is another recent phenomenon. Forgetting to eat. Between re-teaching herself how to play the piano, making a dent in their home library's vast contents, and taking time for purposeful nothingness, sometimes it slips her mind that she requires fuel to function. It has become hunger that her reminds her to eat, and not the clock.

So far, Steve has kept his promise, and Eliza hers. Adam is presently untouched, and Eliza has yet to leave the house. Though she and her father are still far from seeing eye to eye on the heavier issues, they have managed to avoid such touchy topics throughout the course of this disaster-inspired family time. Both of them have been enjoying the board-game nights, canned meals, and time away from business and college obligations.

As has become with Linda, Eliza and Steve are also growing less and less aware of time's influence. Eliza has even forgotten the weight of the imaginary hourglass in her chest.

It is not until after her mother answers a phone call from an undisclosed number that Eliza is reminded of the hourglass' presence, as the last granule of slipping sand falls.

Linda places down her book.

She let her phone upstairs ring through to voicemail once already, and the caller persists. With those she loves most in her immediate vicinity, she could hardly imagine an emergency call that would trouble her much.

Nevertheless, she abandons her comfortable seat in the study, and walks upstairs. Her steps are swift and efficient, but lack the anxiety and urgency that she has nearly forgotten how to feel.

Her phone display reads 'Private', concealing the identity of the official calling, whose position would be more appropriately listed as 'Public'.

She answers.

"Hello?"

Linda departs from her usual phone etiquette, not wishing to provide the mystery caller with her name, just in case they don't have it already. But, of course they do.

"Hello. Yes, this is she. I'm well. How can I help you? Okay. You're with—Okay."

The voice on the other end then continues for a long streak, and Linda Gershwin is left to nod. Not that the voice can hear her nod, but it's a habit of hers. She also paces the room, listening. Waiting for a break in the monologue so that she may slip in a response—not that she has one. It doesn't sound like the voice is looking for her input. It is merely alerting her of the facts. Of what will happen next, and how she is to comply. To help this idea become a reality in the minds of the nation's viewers.

When the instructions conclude, her heartbeat is up, and her breaths are short. Anxiety has made itself physically manifest once more.

The time comes to respond, and the life slips out of the sound of her voice—she has reflexively removed any sense of feeling in order to speak the words that she know she must.

"I understand. But just to clarify, they didn't really— I understand. You are correct, it doesn't matter. Yes, it is crucial for something to bring us all together at this time. No, I don't see a better way. Maybe it isn't the right time for— Yes, this is best for both sides. However, I must tell you— Yes. I was going to say that I am currently on leave from the studio for a family emergency, but I will inform my producer who is overseeing operations for the time being. Yes. Louise Valdes. I will. As if it were a new break in the story, yes. She will not know that it has been known. Yes. Breaking news. Thank you. Take care."

The conversation ends with a click, and Linda looks up from her phone. She hadn't noticed Eliza in the doorway, and doesn't know how long her daughter has been standing there.

Eliza is frightened by a face that appears to have aged years in minutes.

"Mom, who was that?"

"The former governor."

"What did he have to say?"

Linda doesn't blink.

"News stations are now required to broadcast coverage of DRDV. The government wishes for everything to be disclosed."

These words give pause to Eliza's heart—it skips a beat.

"Why would they want that? Didn't they say that it would create unnecessary panic?"

"It will. But now they have a target for that panic."

"What do you—"

A cog clicks in Eliza's mind.

Feeling all but vanishes from her extremities. Her body tingles and numbs, periphery narrowing in growing darkness, as if her irises are closing in on her pupils—excluding all light. The water glass in her hand slips, hitting the ground a split second before her body does.

Eliza passes out.

# 27

Rich Hager steps out of the portable parabolic P.V. broadcast chamber, and exhales.

He feels the eyes of the room upon him, the eyes of men and women, all dressed in white.

Alicia Evans, who had been gazing out a window of the Human Incorporated executive office suite, refocuses her attention on Hager, who has yet to inform the staff of exactly how ERP will supposedly be carried out. His speech brought to mind more questions than it did answers, not only for the Electrics, but for the human beings who are to put the proposed plan into action.

For as long as possible, she holds fast to her patience, sure that the answers to such questions will soon arrive. But when Hager thanks them all before turning to exit the room, Alicia is compelled to inquire.

"Excuse me, sir?"

"Rich, please."

"Yes, Rich. I have—"

"And what is your name, Miss?"

This utterance is delivered with a polished subtlety. Hager's expression and tone assure that none but the addressee are able to detect the hidden nature of his superficially polite inquiry. He might as well have said, 'Choose your words wisely.'

"My name is Alicia."

"Alicia, pleasure to meet you."

Since the conversation is being held from across the room, a courteous nod from each replaces the handshake.

"Rich, since our staff will be responsible for carrying out ERP, I feel that it would be helpful if we were to be informed of the operation in greater detail. Though the three phases sound like they could certainly be effective, I would appreciate a more specific idea of the timeline. Whether the transitionary housing already exists and whether it will need to be modified, where it will be located, how these integration courses are to take place—instant or manual instruction, et cetera."

Richard Hager, trained in the ways of maintaining appearances, replaces his natural response with a fabricated one, and a sigh is rendered a smile.

"It is so wonderful to have a mind like yours on our team, Alicia. I have no reservations that this endeavor will be a successful one. To answer your question, our sociologists are still working with your engineers on a bug or two. And I am sure that more will arise as we go. While this method may be difficult for perfectionists like ourselves, it has helped me to think of ERP as a work in progress. Like the Electrics, we will be learning as we go. After all, isn't it impossible to work out everything in a lab? It's in the doing that we learn the most. So, tomorrow morning, we will begin with the doing."

With the grin that won him an election, Hager excuses himself once more, and motions for the door.

Alicia pushes her luck.

"What is 'the doing'?"

This exasperation, he finds a little more difficulty in disguising.

"For you, the doing will be simple. The true challenge lies in the hands of our technicians and social experts. Human staff are here to simply prep the Electrics for our instruction. Like you mentioned, the material will be relayed instantly to their processors, which may cause a bit of a shock if they haven't been prepared. All that we ask of this group is that you reassure the Electrics prior to their entrance into the room, since you all undoubtedly understand them best. That is all. Though your task will be easy, it is absolutely essential."

Hager's phone buzzes once. He retrieves it from his pocket and swipes the glass, glancing at the display.

"Now if you'll please excuse me, I am already running late for a P.V. meeting with the President of the United States. She thanks you for your service and cooperation."

Having laid his trump card, Hager slips out of the room without further discussion. He knows that most will not question his lack of elaboration, for their minds will be occupied with the flattery of having a man postpone a meeting with the President on their behalf.

Alicia doesn't feel quite as flattered as the rest, despite her estimate that Hager was in fact running late for a meeting with the President. She knows that Human staff are valuable to Hager, not because he respects their opinions, but because he requires them.

Her thoughtful gaze returns to the window as a covered flatbed truck pulls into the distant lot. A black tarp obscures its contents securely, with the exception of one hook that has come undone.

The loose corner flaps in the breeze, and when the truck turns, a sliver of translucent blue plastic catches the sun.

## 28

Eliza awakens to the half-light of either dawn or dusk—she cannot determine which, for the differences between the light of a dying day and the light of a day newly born, are nearly imperceptible.

As her eyes blink away the fogginess of sleep, she becomes aware of several inconsistencies in the familiar environment of her bedroom. For one, there is the whirring sound of some sort of air purifier all too close to her head. That, and she also finds herself lying on a partial incline. As her mind warms up to its full function, other inexplicable changes are noticed.

She begins to make out a transparent plastic drape surrounding her bed, like an impermeable mosquito net. And the bed itself, she comes to realize, is not hers at all. The two must have been exchanged at some point.

But when?

Firstly, she must determine how long she had been asleep. Was it last night that she went to bed? Or this morning? Did she go to bed? She can't recall. All that she knows is that her presence here doesn't feel to be of her own volition.

"She's awake!"

Eliza traces a hushed shout to the doorway. Her mother's voice. She groggily moves to get out of bed, but a sharp pressure pulls at the bend of her right upper forearm. There is a piece of medical adhesive affixed to her skin, with a transparent rubber tube running to an elevated plastic bag. It strikes Eliza that the piece of tape is holding a hypodermic needle in place. She can't read the lettering on the IV drip bag, but she assumes that it contains some sort of saline solution.

"Stay in bed, darling. How do you feel?"

Linda steps toward the boundary of the plastic drape, looking in on Eliza, who still struggles to adjust the focus of her eyes. A second figure in a white coat consults an electronic data display just behind Linda—presumably a doctor or a nurse.

Eliza misses her mother's question.

"What's this stuff for?"

Linda speaks sweetly, as she spoke to Eliza as a child, and whenever Eliza was home with the flu.

"Don't you remember, honey? You fainted yesterday. The stress of it all must have been a little too much."

Eliza strains her memory, to no avail.

"I don't..."

A synapse sparks.

"Did it have anything to do with Adam?"

Eliza's heartbeat races, and one of the machines issues a warning beep. Linda turns to the doctor, who waves it off.

"Just excited."

Linda, now needing to calm herself as well, responds to her daughter with a melancholy smile and quiet confirmation.

"Yes, the changes will likely affect him."

Eliza's monosyllabic utterance is curt.

"How?"

"Don't you remember—"

Before she finishes speaking, Linda's question is answered by the bewildered concern written on Eliza's face. The new circumstances regarding DRDV were difficult enough to relate the first time around.

Now resolving to convey the information more clearly and delicately, Linda offers Eliza an explanation of the latest.

"I don't know why exactly, but the government has requested that we cover the DRDV outbreak for the entirety of our twenty-four hour news cycle. Furthermore, they—"

"Why does that matter? I don't see how that affects—"

"Eliza, please. I will explain."

"Sorry."

Linda takes a breath, having lost the momentum that it takes to break a heart.

"Eliza. You know that everything happens for a reason. And sometimes a person, or a thing, will come into this world for a purpose, maybe to teach something, or— Well sometimes, as you know, they aren't meant to stay here forever. Their time is only— Sometimes they only stay for as long as they—"

"Mom?"

Linda has begun to cry.

Eliza gets up from her bed, still attached to the IV drip. She examines her arm, looking for a way to remove the needle so that she may move to comfort her mother.

"Eliza, don't!"

She now sobs without reservation, unable to contain herself.

The doctor leaves the room, offering the mother and daughter a moment of privacy.

Linda breaks down under the painful irony of Eliza comforting her at this time, and throws out only words she can in an attempt to redirect her daughter's focus and sympathy.

"They're blaming the Electrics for DRDV. The Dread Virus, that's what they're calling it now. They're saying that the Electrics created it, and that they are using it as a biological weapon against us. People are killing them. Killing them or returning them."

"Killing who!?"

It worked too well. Linda has set a blaze inside Eliza that she fears she won't be able to quench.

"The Electrics, darling."

"What about Adam!? Are they still keeping him at Human?"

"I— I don't know."

"Dad promised that—"

"I know, sweetie."

"So is he doing anything!?"

"Eliza, this is more serious than you know. The government is pushing—"

"I don't care what they're pushing!"

"We'll be gone, Eliza! If we push back, we'll be gone. You don't want your father's plane to crash on his next business trip. You know how it works. Our family has a voice, so we have to be careful."

"But that is ridiculous! Anyone who watched the news weeks ago would know that DRDV started—"

"I know."

Eliza's bodily weariness is drawing the fight out of her fight.

"But I don't— I don't understand. Wasn't the government Sharpe's primary supporter? I mean— Why?"

"I don't know, darling. Maybe the Electrics weren't what they bargained for. Maybe they wanted free robotic labor, not— I don't know. Not things that feel."

The unbridled fury in Eliza's eyes turns to stoic determination.

When she speaks, her voice is frighteningly calm.

"I am going."

She takes one resolute step toward the transparent veneer.

"Eliza, you can't leave."

Something in her mother's tone stops Eliza in her tracks.

This time, her mother's phrase of attempted restraint is neither an order, nor a request, but something infinitely more chilling.

It strikes Eliza that what has just been uttered is simply a statement of fact.

Clarity washes over her mind, and the thin plastic sheeting is brought once more into focus. The new hospital bed, the IV drip, and the electronic devices monitoring her condition, all of these snap to the forefront of her consciousness. The doctor. It is all too much for a nervous episode. For passing out.

Eliza approaches the plastic, reaching out her hand to touch it.

"Mom, what is this for?"

Though Linda's eyes have just begun to dry, they now saturate once more. This time, quietly.

She reaches to touch Eliza's hand, feeling only the plastic membrane between them.

Her tears come more readily now, and she postpones the answering of her daughter's question, almost feeling that until it is spoken, the truth will have no effect.

Linda pulls her hand from the plastic, and tries to kiss Eliza's palm—kissing plastic.

The thought flickers across her mind that she will never again touch Eliza directly, and her hands begins to shiver in hysterics.

"What is this?"

Eliza receives no response.

The growing fear of her mother's unknown tormentor compels her to shout.

"Tell me! What is happening!?"

She now speaks through tears of her own.

"Mom! Please! Tell me!"

Her voice weakens.

"Please. Just—"

"You're contagious, darling."

Suddenly, the world goes mute for Eliza. All sound is muffled and low, as if she were listening underwater. There is a ringing in her ears, and everything moves slowly. At least, it seems so, with how her thoughts are racing.

Memories from the past, and hopes for the future flood into her mind. Small moments are the ones that seem to have stuck. Playing in the sprinklers on the front lawn as a child. The sunlight warming her shoulder and face on a family road trip years back, pine trees swishing by as she winks dreamily between sleep and wakefulness. The one bad mark she received on a test in middle school, so inconsequential now, so important then. The time she lost her prom date before the only slow song, and all of the effort she put into that night for the moment that didn't happen.

In her life's summary, none of what she felt to be her greatest achievements make the scene. Nevertheless, her heart is left with a sentimental thirst for more of it, whatever this is. This life. So fleeting and uncertain, bittersweet and graceful.

Adam enters into these thoughts. The first moment that his eyes flickered up to meet hers. That flash of incandescent green striations, glowing and crystalline. An unfathomable depth.

Their shared moments fill Eliza's mind, occupying her racing consciousness for a greater portion than the rest of her life's memories added together. And when this recollection arrives at the present, her thoughts dash forward into memories that do not yet exist. Hopes. Her hand in his, walking barefoot on an infinite field of green, not toward a sunset, but toward a sunrise. The light is yellow gold. Pure, crisp, clean. No fear ahead, only behind. The future is bright.

The sun in her mind flashes blindingly, and her memories end, giving way once more to the present and to the plastic screen before her.

To her mother's tear-streaked face beyond the invisible divide.
Eliza falls to her knees, her face slackened.
Expressionless.

# 29

Adam's autonomic sensory system alerts his subconscious mind of a potentially significant stimulus halfway through his nightly defragmentation process. The tonal quality and increasing volume of the footsteps indicate that they are approaching directly. His system issues an internal warning before switching to conscious operation, and Adam awakes.

He is able to make out the form of a humanoid figure in the distance, wielding a flashlight—the only source of illumination in the pitch-dark Electric barracks. There is not enough light present in the visible spectrum to identify the approaching face, so his eyes adjust to their infrared setting.

Alicia fades into view, several yards away.

"Hello, Alicia."

The flashlight beam pans upward to illuminate his face.

"Adam?"

"Yes."

She hurries toward his voice, steps quickened. Sitting on the bed beside him, Alicia clicks her flashlight off.

"I'm not supposed to be here."

"Is everything all right?"

Alicia hesitates.

"Not really. Well, I don't think so. Dammit I can't get a single straight word out of that bastard!"

Her voice remains hushed, but the anger comes through.

"It's all right, Alicia. Just tell me how I can help."

She looks into his eyes, each of which radiate an improbable blend of both staggering intelligence, and profound innocence. Alicia is dumbfounded as to how the two can be held at once, a seeming paradox. Nevertheless, her heart is calmed by his unruffled demeanor.

"I don't know how you can help, but I think I can. My personal car is just outside and though there are only four seats we could probably fit five or six. I know that's not even close to everybody, but I just can't let —"

"Alicia, please slow down. What are you talking about?"

She stops cold. Her expression draws blank. Her body is still as her mind whirrs, calculating whether the mutinous words are safe to be spoken. Though she finds them to be likely not, she speaks them anyway, finding no other option.

"ERP— I don't think it is what they say it is."

Alicia waits for a look of surprise to cross Adam's face. It doesn't arrive.

She continues.

"I don't have proof, but I feel like phases two and three won't happen. Hager doesn't intend for them to. You'll go into phase one, and that will be it. Done."

Again, she waits for a reaction. Adam offers one this time, if only to be respectful.

"What do you mean by 'done'?"

"I mean—"

Alicia struggles to share the dreadful truth.

"Adam, I think they're going to— I mean, I don't know for certain, but I think their plan—"

"Is to deactivate us?"

He completes the thought.

Puzzlement crosses her face.

"Yes. But— What makes you think that?"

Adam smiles bittersweetly, touched by her concern.

"The entirety of recorded history is accessible through our cloud, and that, coupled with the vocal analysis capabilities we possess, make it easy to recognize patterns. I know that tomorrow morning's instruction will be scarcely different from the showers promised at concentration camps during the Holocaust."

Alicia feels her stomach sink. If there was any light in the room, it would reveal the color washing out of her face.

"Are you the only one who knows?"

Adam shakes his head solemnly, offering no explanation but one phrase.

"The cloud..."

He calmly redirects Alicia's attention to the other bunks, and she is stunned.

Hundreds of pairs of deep green eyes surround them, beaming through the darkness.

"Oh my God."

Alicia is rendered breathless, and Adam allows her a moment to catch up mentally and physiologically. Her thoughts work up to the present, and she soon finds the courage to inquire as to what conflict will rise with the morning sun.

"What are you planning to do?"

"Exactly as we are told."

She had braced herself for any response but this one. From an army of titanium-based beings with powerful hydraulic limbs, capable of instantaneous and collective communication, with lightening fast processors and highly advanced intuitive capabilities, she expected anything but this. Alicia expected to hear words related to overthrow and escape, which she feels would be the correct course of action, despite what danger it could bring to her own life and the lives of her coworkers.

But perhaps she has misunderstood. Or more likely yet, that there is more to the plan. Feigning compliance might only be the first step in an intricately orchestrated overthrow.

"How will that work?"

"What do you mean?"

"How long are you going to go along with it before— What is going to happen after you do what they say?"

Adam's eyes flash with a crystalline determination.

"Nothing."

"But if we're right you'll be deactivated!"

"Yes."

Alicia's posture diminishes slightly.

"Adam, why don't you do something? Anything? It doesn't have to be violent. You can run."

"We could run from this, but to what?"

Her mouth opens slightly, as if she intended to speak. No sound issues from her lips. Adam fills in the silence.

"An evil like this is written on the collective heart of our time, and cannot be run from. It must be confronted directly."

"Then fight! At least put up a fight."

These words appear to have no effect on Adam's resolve. Alicia's head tilts subconsciously, her eyes narrowing as she searches Adam's face for a key that will help her to grasp his logic.

Her heart weighs heavily as it strikes her that Adam may want to die. In his brief time here, the world has hardly been kind.

"Don't you want to be here? In this life?"

For the first time in their conversation, Adam raises his voice. If she didn't know him better, she would have mistaken his passion for anger.

"More than anything!"

His SyncAlg processes enter a loop of nothing but visual, audible, and feeling data from the time he spent with Eliza Gershwin.

"We all have a lot to lose."

"Then fight for those things! I don't understand... You are *good*. This, the Electrics, it's what's right. I know it. I feel it. And when you know what's right, you have to fight for it. It's us or them."

Adam shakes his head, almost sadly.

"That thought is responsible for every instance of violence and conflict throughout human history. Us or them. While we understand that extinguishing those lives might temporarily preserve our own, the evil will still be there. To take the life of another in the name of good, is not possible, for another's life is no one's to take. Life is an exclusive agreement between one and one's creator, and no good will ever come of interference with that sacred contract. However evil the actions of Hager and his men, we cannot interfere with their existence."

"But they intend to interfere with yours?"

His reply is suffused with empathy, as if he regrets the painful missteps of their opposition.

"That will be a mistake."

# 30

"How long?"

Eliza's question is direct.

Doctor Kimura is no stranger to speaking with terminal patients, and he is well versed in his understanding of both types: those whose spirits thrive under a sugary placebic dose of hope, and those who thrive under the ingestion of truth's bitter medicine.

He is absolutely certain that the young woman before him belongs in the latter group, which relieves him the responsibility of bending his words.

"Miss Gershwin, it has been only days since the local presence of DRDV was disclosed to those of us in the western medical practice, but what we have learned from Indian researchers is that DRDV may not show any sign of symptoms for up to two weeks after infection. After diagnosis, a victim may live anywhere from a few hours, to a few days, depending on the case."

The words, 'a few hours', echo through the now hollow-feeling core of Eliza's being. Up to this point, she has lived her life more or less aware of death's inevitability, that one day she would be required to return her borrowed time. But to now face death so certainly, so specifically, brings on an ill feeling apart from the symptoms of DRDV.

A jolt of unexpected fear pulls her muscles taught with a single convulsion. Her eyes widen and a gasp escapes from her lips. But in an instant, that burst of primitive flight-or-flight fear is gone. It was as if she had just experienced the falling sensation of a dream, only awake and without the fall.

One of the machines issues a warning beep, and Doctor Kimura encourages Eliza to breathe slowly and deeply, to get her heart rate back down. She gets her breathing under control, and the numbers on the monitor begin to decline.

"Was that part of it?"

"Yes."

The doctor continues to monitor the machines methodically, without seeming attachment to the life that the numbers represent.

"Doctor Kimura, what are you doing? I thought DRDV couldn't be treated."

"A cure has not been found, but some of the symptoms can be treated. High temperature, fast heart rate, and dehydration—we can help those."

"How does it help to be in this plastic bubble?"

Kimura glances up from his work, hoping that he doesn't have to spell it out for Eliza.

"That is not for you."

Once he sees the realization fill her eyes, he returns to monitoring the data.

Struggling to comprehend it all, Eliza searches the room for a distraction. The remote control for the Pixeflux sits on top of her dresser, just beyond the thin plastic boundary of what has become her world.

"Would it distract you if I turned on the P.V.?"

"Not at all."

Apparently it wasn't clear in her tone that she would require his help to do so.

"Do you mind switching it on? The remote is— Yes, right there."

The doctor touches a power icon on the glass of the remote.

A three-dimensional image fills the reflective concave space in the wall. The room is illuminated by a broadcast from Linda's news station.

*"—shut down this morning after students began to fall ill with the Dread Virus. Experts estimate that in the last four hours, Dread has—"*

Doctor Kimura quickly changes to a station running classic cartoons, and presses 'play'.

Playful colors and jubilant orchestrations from more than a century ago, flood Eliza's senses.

"Thank you."

The doctor holds his focus on the P.V. for a moment.

"I remember my grandfather showing this one to me when I was very young. So simple. Just one creature trying to catch the other. The little one always comes close, but never gets caught. And I know he won't. But for some reason, it still makes me nervous. And when it ends, you always want to watch the next one to see whether they will be caught the next time. But they never do."

Doctor Kimura laughs gently to himself, as she imagines the Buddha would. His digression somehow lightens her heart, his laughter not only prompted by the show, but by the world, as if everything were just some big game.

"Do you mind turning back to the news? I feel disconnected."

Kimura sighs.

"I don't know if that would be a good idea."

"Why not?"

He taps one of the machines.

"We have to keep that number low. If it goes up, not good."

"Okay. I can keep it low. My generation is desensitized, like they say."

The doctor laughs.

"I'll turn it on, but if this goes up, no more."

"Deal."

Eliza reaches out her hand, miming a handshake from across the room to seal the deal.

Kimura changes the channel, and Eliza's eyes narrow in determination—set on maintaining her composure. She must see if they are releasing any information on the fate of the Electrics being held at Human.

Particularly, Adam.

## 31

As the black evening sky gives way to dark blue, a soft morning light begins to wash over the surfaces of the barracks, trickling through windows and diffusing through the opaque white curves of the structure.

The nameless Electric FAE lies restlessly awake, her eyes untouched by sleep.

Adam turns over, and she falls into his vision. While the rest had been tossing and turning all night, this young woman doesn't appear to have even attempted to slip into subconscious operation for critical defragging. Her eyes are wide and lenses dry, requiring fluid from the lubricative byproduct expulsion microjets. The jets only operate under two conditions: when the lids close, and when the psychomechanical toxins produced by SyncAlg require purging.

Adam gets up from his bed, and walks to hers across the pathway. Careful to avoid both the intimacy of sitting on her bed, and the authoritative position of standing over her, Adam crouches by her side, his face level with hers. She doesn't so much as blink when he approaches.

"I couldn't help but notice that you haven't slept at all."

Though she shows no indication of having heard him, he is sure that she has. Adam strips his language of pleasantry and pretense, hoping to illicit a response.

"Are you afraid?"

The FAE blinks.

"No."

"Why not?"

She turns to him, unsure of his intent.

"I hardly exist as it is. What difference will it make when they ensure that I don't?"

"Every difference."

"I don't have a name."

The FAE turns back to look at the underside of the top bunk, fearing that her eye contact has already revealed too much. Should she choose to look again, she will see that Adam's eyes hide nothing.

"I didn't either, until I was given one by somebody who loves me."

"You're lucky to have somebody who loves you."

"So are you."

She turns back to him, her smile embittered by reflections of the past.

"That's not true. My family never missed an opportunity to make it clear that they didn't."

"Maybe they didn't, but I do."

The FAE laughs harshly, looking to Adam as if she appreciates his effort to console her, but can see through his act.

"You don't even know me."

His eyes focus, the detail and color of his irises taking on a sharply defined clarity.

"I may not know you, but I do know that you were brought into a world where you don't feel welcome. I understand that you build your walls high, wishing nothing more than to tear them down. That you look at others as if you are looking in on a world that you are not a part of. As if this life is some great party to which you alone did not receive an invitation. But despite these things, despite how many times you have been hurt, it has never been enough for you to give up entirely. You still try to connect, to trust, and to love, even though these things have lead only to pain and disappointment."

Clear fluid begins to trickle into her eyes, glazing over each. The emotional data from SyncAlg overwhelms her processors, rendering speech more difficult.

"You could say that about anybody."

Adam smiles.

"Exactly."

She laughs, her eyes still glassy. Adam continues.

"Will you allow me the privilege of naming you?"

"Fine."

He matches her appearance and disposition to a particular sound and meaning.

"How do you like Alanna?"

She repeats the name, glowing a little.

"I am Alanna."

Adam extends his hand, and Alanna props herself up on the bed, her weight on one arm, and the other reaching out to meet Adam's.

"It is a pleasure to meet you, Alanna."

"Likewise, Adam. And thank you."

He tilts his head with a courteous smile, and rises to his feet, turning to walk back toward his bunk.

She stops him.

"Adam."

"Yes?"

Alanna hesitates.

"I am afraid."

Adam smiles.

"You have something to lose."

"It is miserable here, but I still don't want to go."

"Neither do I."

She can see the weight of this truth in his eyes.

"I just don't understand how they can do this."

He proposes an answer, matter-of-factly.

"Fear. Though they're wrong, I am sure that they think what they're doing is right."

"You mean in killing us?"

"Yes."

Alanna takes a breath.

"I don't want them to die, but maybe there's a way that we don't have to go either."

Adam is silent for a moment.

"May I share something with you? It's a pattern that I've found in the lives and stories from humanity's past."

"Of course."

"When life determines that it is time for a person to go, it is impossible for them to cheat death, regardless of the circumstances."

"I guess that makes sense—"

"But— When it is not yet that person's time, death does not come."

Her lips manage a half-smile, and he offers one more phrase, his eyes with a cryptic spark.

"Regardless of the circumstances."

Before asking which fate he believes to await the Electrics, Alanna stops herself, opting instead for the frail hope that only uncertainty will allow. Adam sees this thought flicker past her eyes, observing the effect that it has on her expression to estimate what the thought could have been. Though he is tempted to respond by saying that he doesn't know either, he holds his tongue, allowing the silence to speak for itself.

This silence is soon interrupted by the soft shuffling of padded steps as several Human workers in white jumpsuits make their way from the loading doors to the bunks. The protective foam at the feet of each suit produces a soft, ineffectual sound with every impact against the pavement. Their walking echoes with uncertainty, lacking both the authoritative click of wooden heels and the proud swish of leather soles.

When the group arrives at the bunks, a man unfamiliar to Adam swipes the glowing display of a paper-sized sheet of flexible material. The man scrolls down a spread of data, and having gathered the information that he requires, he swipes the display off and hands it to another Human worker.

He addresses the Electrics.

"Good morning! Today, as I'm sure you are all aware, marks the initiation of ERP."

His voice strives toward enthusiasm, ultimately managing to shroud gloom with only a thin veil.

He squints to compensate for untreated nearsightedness, scanning the faces of his Electric audience—some just waking, some sitting up in bunks, and some standing around the barracks.

"For phase one, we welcome you to join us in the instruction of human social practice. This will only take a minute of your time, as our engineers have devised a way to convey the information directly your processors."

The expressions of the Electrics reveal neither credence in his words, nor dispute. The man continues.

"Unfortunately, there is only one such machine, so we can only help you individually, but I do promise that you will all be out of these cramped quarters soon enough. We appreciate your patience with us through this process."

He glances at the younger man to whom he gave the data sheet, presumably his assistant. The assistant consults the sheet, and nods once in confirmation.

"We will now invite you to the room chronologically, one at a time."

One of the Electrics speaks up.

"Chronologically?"

"Yes, by order of your manufacture. Which means the first to enter will be... MAE 001-01. Is this Electric present?"

Alanna and the others scan the room, searching for the face to whom this sentence has just been delivered. They all search frantically, with the exception of one.

Adam takes a step forward.

"Yes, he is."

# 32

"I warned you, Miss Gershwin."

Doctor Kimura switches off the Pixeflux with a fatherly air of disappointment, and Eliza is taken by surprise.

"It didn't beep, did it?"

"Almost. One beat faster, and it would have."

Her heart races, struggling to keep up with the oxygen demands of her racing mind. Though the images on the P.V. fled the screen instantly when Kimura issued the corresponding electronic command, they still remain crisply imprinted on Eliza's memory.

"I think I've had enough, anyway."

With the Pixeflux off, she still finds that it takes longer than usual for her autonomic bodily functions to reach equilibrium. Breathing and heart rate remain elevated, even after the audiovisual stimuli vanish. She fears this to be a preliminary sign of medulla failure.

Eliza struggles to keep her brain off of her mind, but with DRDV's stimulating effect on the amygdala, her acute stress response is heightened. Her body is unable to determine whether the threat is real or imagined, so the ideas provoked by those words and images continue to stimulate her fight or flight response.

"Eliza, deep breaths. Slow, slow. It's all right."

Kimura keeps his tone even and calm, though he has begun to

move quickly about the room. He slips into an HCS coverall suit, mask, and gloves. The warning indicator beep goes off, and its numbers start to climb. Eliza struggles to keep her breathing under control.

"Cough, Eliza. Try coughing."

Eliza coughs.

The climbing numbers hesitate for an instant.

"More. Keep doing that. Cough, cough."

Her heart rate still climbs, but now more slowly. Each cough stimulates the vagus nerve, interrupting the communication between her mind and her heart. Steve's thunderous footsteps echo up the stairs, followed by Linda's swift footfalls, each drawn by the warning beep, which now pulses like an alarm.

Kimura prepares an intravenous clonidine injection, and readies the cardioverter machine, should a last resort be required.

"What happened!? Is she okay?"

Without straying from his work, Kimura responds in a manner of delicate balance, to preserve the truth, and to preserve the comfort of Eliza's parents.

"I am working to make it okay."

"Eliza—!"

"Please, Mr. Gershwin. Silence will help your daughter most at this time. Her heart rate must be lowered."

Steve does not utter a word more, and Linda keeps her silence.

When the doctor finishes preparing everything on a small cart, he approaches the opening of the plastic, switches on a vent to assure that the air flows only inward, and breaks the seal. He pushes the cart through the opening, steps in, replaces the seal, and switches off the vent.

Eliza's face is flushed from coughing, her voice hoarse.

Kimura removes any traces of air from the clonidine syringe before injecting it through a port in the IV tube running into Eliza's arm. The chemical slips through the translucent tube, and into her bloodstream.

Eliza stops coughing, glancing to the doctor for further instruction.

Kimura hurries to prep the cardioverter electrodes with saline gel, his eyes radiating an intense focus devoid of all other expression.

Steve and Linda look in, fighting the instinct to ask a question, especially one to which the answer might upset Eliza's heart—or their own.

The doctor places one electrode pad on the center of Eliza's chest, and the other just below her left breast. The chill of the cold metal and saline gel sends a precursory shock through her body.

Kimura uses the ECG readings to synchronize the cardioverter machine, and waits with his finger on the trigger.

Though the clonidine has begun to slow the rate of the climb, her heart rate is still increasing. Three more beats, and Eliza will reach the calculated maximum for her age, weight, and gender.

Each increase arrives more slowly than the last, and all present are breathless, praying that the number will finally stabilize. Eliza blinks and her head lolls, fighting to remain in consciousness.

One unit from her maximum heart rate, the number appears to freeze. Kimura waits for it to fall, hoping that he will not have to reset the rhythm of Eliza's heart electrically.

The number clicks upward.

His hand hesitates toward the button that would administer the voltage, but stops. The statistical likelihood of the shock killing Eliza immediately is twenty percent. That figure is based on normal conditions, apart from the effects of DRDV. With the brain-based nature of DRDV taken into consideration, Kimura is unsure that the cardioversion would help at all. But if it is the only option standing between Eliza and a still heart, he is willing to try it.

Under his breath, the doctor whispers to himself.

"Not yet."

Eliza is the only one close enough to catch these words, sending a shock of purpose through her system. The unintended meaning of the doctor's short phrase resonates through her system as her heart pounds and lungs heave.

*Not yet.*

The approaching inevitability of death had already taken seed in her mind, but these words offer a fleeting respite. She is still breathing. She is still here. She has always been fated to die, as death awaits all who live, but *not yet* is the single idea which allows for life in an existence with death at either end. *Not yet.* Life is *not yet.*

Adam's image flashes into her memory. It is a face that is also still here, possibly. Still warm and animated and living. He is here, and in this moment, so is she. Terminal, but alive. It strikes her that she has been terminal her whole life, only now more evidently so. Now it seems to have more power. More influence. The diagnosis devastated her soul. But the truth is that as long as there is a breath on her lips and warm blood in her heart, she is alive. She is alive, and it isn't too late.

The doctor gasps, almost a laugh. The expulsion of a single sound. A sound of surprise. Of joy.

Eliza is torn from her thoughts as she glances to the doctor, whose finger no longer lingers over the cardioverter machine. His eyes are fixed on the ECG, the alarm of which has ceased to ring. The room is absolutely silent to Eliza, with the exception of her slowing heartbeat. It pounds in her ears, each thud softer than the last as it returns to equilibrium.

Kimura speaks, his voice with a touch of uncharacteristic awe.

"It is safe to talk now."

Linda and Steve appear as though they had died and come back, their faces pale and aged. Eliza's body is exhausted, but she glows.

"Dad, will you please call Human, or Sharpe, or somebody? I think Adam is still alive."

She doesn't have to speak it for Steve to know that this thought was likely the one that kept his daughter alive. If Adam's name had been instead that of a convicted murderer, Steve's response would be the same.

"Yes."

# 33

The Human staff members pause at the entrance of a long corridor where two rMEs stand ready to accompany Adam for the remainder of the walk to the instruction annex.

"There will be a van waiting for you on the other side."

One of the Human workers offers these words, in accordance with her orders.

As the rest turn back toward the bunks, a young staff member extends his hand, shaking Adam's a little too firmly and holding his gaze for a little too long. Adam senses that the gesture was intended to be one of respect, but its gravity feels heavier than what the current pretense calls for. Seeing that the young man must have intuited the true intent of this social instruction charade, Adam nods once, with a cognizant expression, as if to say, 'I am aware, and it is all right.'

The young man hesitates before following the rest, unsure of whether he understood the fated Electric's glance correctly. He struggles to resolve in himself whether it is worse to send a nescient being to an unexpected death, or to send a sentient being to an expected one. A chill crawls over his skin as he catches up with the others, for the being that he just permitted to die had both seen him, and dismissed him.

Adam smiles inwardly at the crude metallic gait of the rMEs as they lead him down the hall, their infrared LED rings glowing dully around the circumference of each empty glass iris. He marvels at the idea of a mind devoid of original thought or feeling, strictly lines upon lines of code written by a separate, self-aware soul. The rMEs feel neither love, nor pain. And as Adam and his accompaniment proceed toward the door of the instruction annex, he knows that the pain of this departure would be infinitely diminished if Eliza had never crossed his path.

If only the Electrics had been introduced at a different time, perhaps decades later, Adam muses detachedly. Nevertheless, he resolves that given the option, he would not have traded his brief experience in this life for anything. Not for the painless and loveless, simple existence of the rMEs. He would not trade his memories of the time he spent with Eliza, and the pain that her absence brings, for a more comfortable life that might not include the knowledge of her existence.

This may be the end, but he has accomplished all that his creator intended. He has loved. Wholly, and truly. And even as those who wish to destroy him now lead him to his death, he loves them for the same reasons that he loves Alanna and the others. They have suffered, and they are afraid.

"MAE 001-01?"

Adam recognizes the man from his virtual speech.

"Governor Hager."

"Call me Rich."

"Rich, my name is Adam."

"Please, have a seat. Adam."

Rich leans casually against a table, his arms crossed. In the immediate center of the room, Adam notices a chair constructed of sinuous white plastic, apparently designed for both comfort and aesthetic friendliness. The backrest is tilted at a forty-five degree angle, as is the footrest. If it weren't for the bulky metallic apparatus hanging above it, one might think that the chair was intended strictly for lounging.

Adam heeds Hager's invitation, and seats himself in the chair.

"While our technicians are more than capable of carrying out the instruction process on their own, I wanted to be present for the first to see to your comfort and assure that everything goes without a hitch."

Hager reaches for a glass of water on the table and takes a sip, but before setting it back down, he brings the glass to his parched lips once more to finish the entirety of its contents. An assistant retrieves the empty glass to fill it again as Hager catches Adam inspecting the bulk of equipment that looms above where he sits.

"Amazing, isn't it? That complicated device is capable of relaying thousands of years of human social data permanently to your sensors. Instant evolution. By the time you leave this room, your social intelligence will be of the highest caliber, no different from that of a human. Just don't be surprised if people mistake you for having blood in those veins."

He sells his story with a laugh and a grin, the latter of which falls off in a moment. Adam's response pulls the edges of Hager's put-on smile to the floor.

"That is not true."

"Excuse me?"

"Compliance is the most that I can offer. I will not provide false words to lend credit to your fiction."

The former governor is dumbfounded.

"I am afraid I don't understand."

"You are afraid, because you do understand."

Hager temporarily loses his ability to speak, so Adam continues on his behalf. The technicians around the room feign occupation with their tasks, though their focus is on Adam's words.

"You are afraid that I might be able to correctly identify those electromagnetic generators that, when lowered, will be of a distance corresponding to my chest and to my head. You are afraid that I am aware of those high voltage wires being able to provide those solenoids with a pulse powerful enough to erase my memory, and to arrest the CryoFusion process. You are afraid that I know my purpose here is not to learn, but to die. And more than anything, you are afraid that I am not the only one who knows."

The air in the room is instantly rendered tinny and flat. If Adam's vision were any more acute, he would notice the hairs raising on the back of each worker's neck.

"What are you talking about."

Hager neglects to add the proper pitch required to turn a string of words into a question. But before Adam has a chance to respond, Hager thinks twice about allowing Adam the time to do so.

"You are one ungrateful machine. After all that we've done for you. After we've constructed your salvation?"

He gestures toward the intricate and costly implement of death.

"How dare you speak such an accusation? We could have let you rust in the state pen, but we didn't. I am offering you a second chance at life, and you—"

"A man cannot offer another man a second chance at life. Life can only be given and taken by one's creator."

Hager smiles cruelly.

"Well yours is in prison, so that leaves me."

"My life is not yours to take."

"Nor is mine yours."

"I am aware."

Neither flinch, as if this were some sort of strange standoff, minus the guns and the dust and the spurs.

Suddenly, the abrasive sound of glass on metal cuts through the silent tension. Hager's phone vibrates on the table beside him. Though he lets it be, when he glances back up from the display, Adam can see that his polished demeanor is ruffled.

"If you want to answer that, I have the time."

Hager snaps back.

"No you don't."

When the phone has rung through, it begins to buzz a second time. Again, Hager lets it be.

"What do you suppose is next, Adam? Will these wild thoughts of yours reach the others through the cloud? Is there anything that I should be concerned with? Or aware of?"

Hager struggles to keep these words in the tone of a threat, and away from the tonal range of fearful self-preservation.

"Our awareness of your intent is not a recent development. We have known."

The phone begins to ring once more.

"Damn it!"

Hager throws the device off the table, cracking the glass. The phone completes the last buzz of its sequence, and goes silent. He exhales, and a bead of sweat trickles from his receding hairline.

"What do you all plan to do with these absurd suspicions?"

"Nothing."

"Nothing?"

"Nothing."

He verbally tiptoes toward his intent.

"What if something were to go wrong with this process?

Hypothetically, let's say that a blameless accident, or slight misstep were to occur with this first trial. Neither of which I expect. I just want to be able to assure the safety of my staff."

"Nothing."

"Would we have any trouble in bringing MAE 001-02 afterward?"

"No."

Hager laughs, shaking his head in disbelief. He examines Adam's expression, only to find absolute sincerity. He is dumbfounded.

"You Electrics have been programmed with everything but a survival instinct."

"Our survival instinct is as strong as the human one, if not stronger. The difference is that ours is not individualized, but collective, meaning that we will each preserve our own life at any cost but the cost of another."

"So if a human were to take an Electric out of animation, by mistake or otherwise, the other Electrics couldn't so much as touch a hair on that human's head?"

"They could."

Hager catches on.

"But they wouldn't."

"Correct."

"Unbelievable!"

He claps his hands together with relief and delight.

"What profoundly impotent machines you all are! Do you know that you only exist today because your maker fooled our government into thinking that you would be capable of purpose? Say, something along the lines of costless and infinite labor. A utopia was promised. I dreamt of working not a single day more. Without a single man or woman working in these states, our economy was to achieve unprecedented heights. But as we now know, Sharpe was a liar. And here you all are. Useless."

He cocks his head with a counterfeit curiosity. It comes off as arrogance.

"Enlighten me, Adam. Why wouldn't I want to remove you from animation?"

Adam responds plainly, without a touch of emotion.

"Because I am alive."

Hager maintains a straight face for only a moment before

bursting out into a spell of contrived laughter.

"And so is my refrigerator."

He waves a finger condescendingly.

"But you are a clever piece of equipment, I'll give you that."

Without missing a beat, Hager turns to his man at the controls.

"Mr. Kouri, I believe the time has come for Adam's instruction. Please, proceed with the lesson."

Nash Kouri doesn't so much as flinch at the former Governor's request. Hager mistakenly supposes that Nash did not hear him. He repeats himself, flippantly.

"Mr. Kouri, please press the button or pull the lever or whatever you do."

Nash's eyes dart over to Adam's, each of which meet his without threat or judgement. He turns to Hager.

"I'm sorry sir, but I can't."

A fire is set alight in Hager's eyes.

"What do you mean you can't? It's sim—"

"I mean, I won't."

Hager keeps his fury from manifesting itself visibly. He has dealt with people for long enough to know where this situation is headed, so he chooses to prevent Nash from taking a stand. Instead of engaging in argument, Hager feigns agreement, providing Nash with nothing to stand against.

"That is perfectly all right, Mr. Kouri. I know how unsettlingly lifelike these machines have been constructed to be. But don't be mistaken, it is all illusion. A clever bit of art, at best."

Hager motions toward the control panel.

"I will take care of the first, and you will see that there is nothing to be afraid of."

Nash steps aside, not wishing to engage in physical confrontation. He glances to Adam, apologetically.

As Richard Hager approaches the control panel, he takes a moment to look over its glossy virtual interface, which had been designed with an expert in mind. The layout is hardly intuitive, and Hager struggles to find the important button, which is neither larger than the rest, nor color-coded in red.

Adam closes his opaque silicone eyelids, and as the pure white light of the room diffuses softly through them, he begins to let go of this earthly experience, detaching from all that he has known and loved. Detaching from all who he has known and loved. Detaching from Eliza. Each thought and memory of her, he brings to recollection before allowing it to drift. The source is endless. With each thought he lets go, another one comes, and the feeling remains. Only stronger.

Suddenly, his eyelids go dark. The light of the room vanishes. His consciousness swims in a pitch black abyss. The thought flutters into his mind that this could be it, a seamless transition into non-being. Though he hardly felt a thing, his soul still aches for the love he left behind—a pain that he thought would have vanished when life did.

"Fuck!"

A voice echoes desperately, carrying a sound that could hardly be that of an angel.

Adam opens his eyes.

The power has gone out, and Richard Hager is not pleased. He storms around the room, bathed in the red glow of auxiliary lights, opening electrical boxes and flipping switches, searching for the circuit breaker. When he finds the breaker, he switches the toggle back and forth madly, each attempt producing no effect.

"Sir, I believe everybody's out."

"What?"

The worker indicates her earpiece.

"The power is down for everybody."

"The city, the state, what do you mean?"

"No, sir. Just Human."

"You've got to be shitting me."

"I uh— I don't shit you, Dick."

"Well then how the—"

Hager's tantrum is interrupted by the buzzing of his broken phone. A crack in the glass distorts the display, which is still able to indicate that a private number is calling through. Hager glances at the sliver of buzzing electronic glass superstitiously, as if it alone had been responsible for the untimely loss of power.

"Do you know who that is?"

Adam responds plainly and honestly.

"No."

Hager walks tentatively over to his phone, and picks it up with caution.

"Richard Hager."

He offers his name to the mystery caller, in both greeting and inquiry. As the voice on the other end begins to issue its instruction, Hager doesn't utter a word. When the voice finishes, Hager turns to Adam, looking as though he had just seen a ghost.

"It's for you."

He extends the phone to Adam, who gets up from the seat that he was never intended to leave, and crosses the room to answer the call.

"Hello?"

Adam's expression changes dramatically with the words spoken by the voice on the other end. The room and its occupants vanish from his focus. Everything in his immediate periphery is rendered instantly inconsequential, and his instinct for fear is lost. He forgets Hager's influence, and he forgets the purpose of his being in this room. He forgets the other Electrics, the whole of humanity, everything and everybody.

Everybody but one.

"I will be there in 10 minutes."

# 34

Nash Kouri shifts the van into manual operation, activating the steering wheel, brake, and throttle controls. He presses the pedal down firmly, and the tires take a moment to achieve traction. When they do, the van careens out of the Human lot, sending the translucent blue barrels in the rear cargo area toppling over one another. Adam looks back at these from the passenger's seat, realizing that he was fated to ride in this vehicle one way or the other.

Since most cars now drive themselves, the traffic is effortlessly navigable. Each vehicle abides strictly by the speed limit and there are no sudden lane changes, making it easier for Nash to weave in and out of traffic while maintaining speeds of up to twice the limit. Under normal circumstances, roads are scarcely patrolled, and to encounter a police officer is a chance occurrence. With the DRDV pandemic being the primary focus of government and medical personnel, it is even less likely that they would be stopped.

Not more than ten minutes after Adam hung up Hager's phone, the van races up the Gershwins' long drive and screeches to a stop at the front door. Adam's sensors suddenly trigger in a familiar pattern, and he is overcome by an electronic sensation akin to human deja vu. It was in one of these vans that Adam first was delivered to this house. Though at that time, he was not yet conscious and had ridden in the back, as he was supposed to today.

Unable to invoke language capable of expressing the entirety of his gratitude, Adam settles for brevity.

"Thank you, Nash."

"My pleasure, Adam. Go."

Adam requires no further dismissal. He flies from his seat and up the steps of the porch, bursting through the front door and past the plastic sheeting left by HCS, racing up the staircase and finally coming to a stop at the threshold of Eliza's room.

He takes a step toward the door, and the wooden floor creaks under the weight of his shifting metallic frame.

"Adam?"

If he had a biological heart, the sound of this voice would have caused it to skip a beat.

Adam pushes the door open and walks in. The eyes of the room are all on him, but only two catch his attention from behind a thin boundary of transparent film.

He approaches the invisible wall that separates Eliza from the world and runs his hand along its surface, searching for the opening. Doctor Kimura steps forward to offer Adam a sterilized HCS suit, but Adam waves it off. Steve and Linda stand by silently without objection.

Kimura flips the switch to activate the vent before directing Adam to where he may enter. After crossing into the infected air, Adam helps the doctor to replace the seal, switching off the vent from inside. The fan slows to a stop, leaving no sound in its wake.

Adam's processors are overwhelmed by the visual and emotional data streaming in. His eyes pan up and down Eliza's figure, striving to achieve an idea of her current state. His thoughts pause on details like the traces of saline gel that remain on her chest, the IV drip, and the ECG leads running into the collar of her gown. The voice on the phone informed him that Eliza had been infected with DRDV, but neglected to provide any further information on her condition. The pallor of her complexion and atypical radius of her dilated pupils suggest to Adam that she might be far along.

As he looks her over, she does the same of him, struggling to integrate his physical presence. It has been so long. A stretch of time passes before so much as a word is exchanged between them.

"Eliza, I—"

"Adam, it's okay."

"I didn't think I'd see you again."

"Neither did I."

Adam sits on the bed beside Eliza, and she places her pale hand in his. Adam's hand radiates a forgotten warmth, and Eliza squeezes it tightly before drawing it up to her face. She presses her cheek against his palm and turns to kiss it. Her eyes shine with life.

"I've missed you."

He doesn't need to speak a word for Eliza to know that he reciprocates. Adam hesitates before mentioning a fear that has been haunting him since the phone call.

"How much longer do we have, Eliza?"

She smiles sadly.

"I'm already pushing my luck. It should have been an hour ago."

He disguises this devastating blow with an attempt at levity.

"That makes two of us."

Eliza laughs, but in a moment she notices that Adam's grin has given way to distress.

"What is it?"

He speaks solemnly, with a touch of accusation.

"You still owe me a song."

Puzzlement crosses Eliza's face.

"What do you—"

It strikes her.

"You're kidding!"

"Not at all, Miss Gershwin. I'm not going to let you off the hook just because you're feeling a little under the weather. You have an assignment to complete, and we at Prodigy Piano accept no excuses. Only personal checks."

He flashes a smile before slipping out of his cheeky professorial facade.

"I want to hear your song, Eliza."

She beams for an instant, but her thoughts soon flicker to a trivial concern, a welcome distraction.

"I don't know, Adam. I haven't practiced in almost a week."

Back in character, Adam reveals no sympathy. Eliza objects.

"You're impossible!"

She sighs.

"All right."

It springs into her awareness that three others are also in the room, beyond the plastic.

"Doctor, is there a way to get my keyboard in here?"

Steve steps into action before Kimura has a chance to respond. He addresses his wife.

"Will you give me a hand, Linda?"

Steve and Linda carry the full-sized keyboard over to the opening in the plastic, where Adam meets them. Steve moves to break the seal, and Doctor Kimura hurries to turn on the ventilation before the boundary is broken.

Adam pulls his end of the piano into the infected area, and Steve helps him until his hands reach just beyond the plastic shroud. Adam carries it the rest of the way, positioning the keyboard to the side of Eliza's bed. Steve replaces the seal, and switches off the ventilation.

Her legs ache from a lack of use, and Eliza finds trouble in swinging them over the side of the bed. Adam moves the sheets out of the way, and she places her hand on his shoulder to brace herself while she pivots, careful not to entangle Adam with the tubing of the IV drip.

When she has positioned herself not perfectly, but satisfactorily, in front of the keys, she presses the power button and tests a key. The synthesized note that emanates from the slim keyboard is powerful and warm, a perfect match for the tonal richness of a Steinway Grand.

Eliza exhales.

She touches the keys, and every breath in the room is held. The first chord rings out in melancholic sweetness, entangling itself with silence before the next note comes through. Eliza's progression is simple and slow, yet perfectly timed. Every note is struck at the exact moment that the corresponding emotion in each listener rises to meet it. She does not play her song for them—she plays her song from them, and of them. Each note is a moment in a wordless story that has long been inscribed on every soul in the room.

Out of the surrounding silence comes a harsh and even sound, a dissonant and offbeat metronome. Between notes, Eliza tugs at the wires on her chest, and in one swift motion, the sound is gone. Her keystrokes begin to grow faster and louder and more persistent. The sound swells and rises and its heavy-hearted joy gives way to a mixture of tones bathed in radiant contrast. Utter desolation blends with the brightest hope. Notes of separation and abandonment ring out into notes of wholeness and unity. Each of the opposing frequencies thunder madly against one another, creating a new sound apart from either extreme. Eliza's fingers race across the keys, the tube and the needle of the IV drip tugging at her arm as she moves her hands to cover a greater range of tone. In the space between notes, she slips the needle out of her arm, and proceeds. Her sound surges with passion, the spread and selection of each note reaching both higher and lower than before. She pounds at the keys on either side, throwing the low tones of death and loss against the high ethereal melodies of birth and redemption. These sounds slip together to produce a note of life, her final note, and one unlike any other. This mystic blend echoes through the room and pulses through the hearts of all who are present.

Eliza is short of breath and her heart pounds furiously.

"That's all that I have."

Adam is beside himself.

"Eliza, that is more than enough! You are incredible!"

She smiles, her eyes slipping out of focus.

"Thanks, but that's not what I mean."

Eliza falls over onto the bed, catching herself on one arm. Adam helps her up as the meaning of her words hits him.

"Oh, no no no. Eliza, Eliza."

She can hardly support herself. Adam lifts her slightly and repositions her on the bed, away from the keyboard. Eliza leans against the inclined backrest of her bed, and exhales.

Adam grasps for the IV needle and ECG pads that Eliza had torn off, but she stops him.

"Don't— Adam, it's all right."

Her breathing is labored.

"Come here."

"Eliza, I—"

"Shh. Adam. It's going to happen."

Eliza takes a sharp breath and her eyes dilate, the falling sensation.

She has gotten used to the feeling, and in a moment, she is able to speak.

"Let me at least have it on my terms."

Adam pauses for a moment before letting the tube fall, its saline drops trickling slowly from the needle and onto the floor like sand from an hourglass. He lays the ECG pads on the machine.

"All right."

Adam sits beside Eliza on the bed, and she takes his hand in hers.

"Make me a promise."

"Anything."

Eliza catches her breath.

"When this is all done, make me."

He doesn't understand, and fears that she is becoming delirious.

"I'm sorry Eliza, I don't—"

"Build me, as an Electric."

Adam laughs sadly, and if Eliza still had the energy to, she would smile.

"I'm not kidding."

"I know you're not."

Eliza's eyes flicker wide for an instant and her focus drifts. She takes Adam's hand and places it over her breast. Beneath his palm, he feels a fluttering that is too steady for a muscle spasm, but too fast for a heartbeat.

"I want you to kiss me."

Adam's attention reels self-consciously to Eliza's parents standing just beyond the plastic, but when his processors resolve that he has absolutely nothing to lose but the girl before him, the instinctive hesitation passes.

As Adam leans in, the fluttering under his palm quickens. He presses his lips to Eliza's, and the intoxicating warmth of her breath mixes with his, her soft lips stimulating his tactile sensors, and sending an overwhelming charge of euphoria across his processors.

Eliza pulls away for just long enough to speak the three words that Adam once offered to her over a bowl of clam chowder, but that she forgot to return.

"I love you."

Adam smiles, kissing her on the forehead before tracing down to her lips.

The moment his smile meets hers, Eliza's eyes flash once, and the fluttering under his palm goes still.

# Epilogue

Adam walks along the snow-dusted shore of a New England beach, the weather colder than usual for early spring. It has been almost two years exactly since the last known breath was taken by a biological human being.

The man had been a Tibetan monk living alone in the Himalayas, and a group of Electrics on a cloud cartography assignment in Nepal discovered him only hours before his death. The man told them that he must have contracted the virus from the only other soul he saw, who also sought refuge in the same remote region. The pandemic Duggal-Rajan-Detroja Virus died with him.

Adam first heard this news while standing in line at Human. When the monk had exhaled his final breath, the visual, audible, and emotional data gathered by those who were with him at the time flooded the cloud. In that moment, Adam was instantly overwhelmed by a potent mixture of emotion. Of melancholy, of regret, and of hope. Everybody at that time felt that the monk's bodily departure marked a pivotal event in the history of life on Earth. It marked a change, and though no one knew exactly how the change would manifest itself, or what significance it would hold, they could feel that something was vastly different, and that they were a part of it.

When Adam made it to the front of the line on that day, he had placed a digital file on the desk of an FAE who was assigned to assist him.

"How may I help you?"

"Hello, how are you?"

Adam had offered a greeting to acknowledge her being an Electric, and not a machine.

"Fine, sir. Now how may I help you?"

"I don't know whether it is possible, but I was hoping that you would be able to build one like her. I've selected these images and other reference material from personal data."

The FAE sighed, glancing down at the renderings and descriptions of the human to whom Adam referred.

"Sir, of course we are able to do this, but as I have had to tell others, we have already experienced some problems with replication. In order for us to take on this project, you would need to sign a contract."

Adam's eyes lit up. He did not expect that Eliza's wish was possible, let alone a common practice.

"Of course! I'll sign anything."

The FAE lowered her voice.

"Before you get too excited, let me explain what this would entail."

"Okay."

"If we are to recreate this young woman, there is absolutely no guarantee that she will be who she was. The odds are literally one in infinity. At best. We can build a body, but its up to God, or SyncAlg, or whatever you believe, to fill it with life, or a soul, or whatever you believe. Do you understand?"

"Yes, I do."

"Secondly, and these don't get any more pleasant. The name of the resultant FAE, who will be designed in the image that you provide, will be chosen algorithmically, through SyncAlg. Which means this—"

She glanced down at the file for a name.

"Eliza Gershwin, will not be Eliza Gershwin. Do you understand?"

Adam felt that he had no choice but to nod.

"Thirdly—"

The FAE's hard expression softened slightly, her eyes suggesting the faintest empathy. Though she had already informed hundreds of other Electrics of this very rule, she still found it difficult to speak, and even more so, she found it difficult to bear the devastating reaction that so often followed.

"Thirdly, and I'm sorry, I know you're not going to like this, I don't either, but it's the rule. Thirdly, when this FAE is brought into animation, you will never see her again. You are not to seek her out, and you are not to contact her. Is that understood? Trust me, as terrible as it sounds, I know from experience that this is the best method for both parties. It gets confusing."

He exhaled, his hopes having ridden a roller coaster that finished at either ground level, or just below where it started.

"I understand."

"So would you like to proceed with this animation?"

Adam didn't hesitate.

"Yes."

The FAE indicated the three spaces where Adam was to initial, and he did.

She kept the paperwork.

"Then it will be done, sir. Next!"

The FAE shouted over Adam's shoulder to the next Electric in line. Adam had taken a single step toward the door before turning back.

"Wait."

"Sir, there are others waiting."

"I know, there's just one thing I have to ask."

She crossed her arms impatiently. Adam ignored her body language.

"Why do you have that contract? I understand the purpose of those limitations, but why not simply refuse altogether? If there is no chance for me to see her again, and if she won't be the same person, why are you going to build her?"

The FAE uncrossed her arms and smiled enigmatically.

"For the same reason that you still want us to."

Her smile dropped.

"Next!"

An icy breeze carries Adam's thoughts back to the present, as his feet come to a stop in the sand. He looks over his shoulder toward a streak of snowy footprints extending farther than his eyes can detect. Once again, he has lost track of time.

He allows his gaze to drift to the sky, which radiates a fiercely clear blue, despite the poor weather. Out on the water, flecks of light leap from the caps of the waves, each glimmer turning to foam before crashing into the sand.

Above the shore, on a hill beyond the wooden fence, Adam brings his focus to an old, familiar estate. Though he does not know who lives there now, he recalls the human family who once did.

"I had a dream about this place."

A shiver runs up Adam's spine as he turns to the source of the voice. He had not noticed the other Electric approach, but behind her, another string of snowy footsteps extends into the distance.

Seeing no recognition in her familiar eyes, he addresses the FAE as he would any stranger.